FALLIN'
FOR A
Jamaican
KING

A NOVEL BY

CANDY MOORE

Curvy Girl Publications is now accepting manuscripts from aspiring & experienced BBW romance authors!

WHAT MAY PLACE YOU ABOVE THE REST:

Heroes who are the ultimate book bae: strong-willed, maybe a little rough around the edges but willing to risk it all for the woman he loves.

Heroines who are the ultimate match: the girl next door type, not perfect - has her faults but is still a decent person. One who is willing to risk it all for the man she loves.

The rest is up to you! Just be creative, think out of the box, keep it sexy and intriguing!

If you'd like to join the Curvy Girl family, send us the first 15K words (60 pages) of your completed manuscript to curvygirlpub@royalty-publishinghouse.com

Synopsis

*S*amantha is living the life every woman could ever dream of, she is married to a successful and handsome man that is loved and respected by everyone in their community. To anyone on the outside looking in she has the perfect life, with the perfect man. But Samantha's life is anything but perfect, her so called perfect life is nothing more than a perfect lie!

Enters the infamous Kingsale Rock. King, as he is known in the streets, is about to come into Samantha's life and show her exactly what she's missing. Being with a Jamaican street King is all Samantha really needs in her life.

King is about to turn Samantha's world upside down in more ways than one!

Prologue

I was always the type of woman that wanted the fairy-tale life. The handsome husband, that loves and adores me, with three beautiful kids. The only thing I've been able to accomplish so far is the handsome husband and nothing else. I'm trapped in a loveless marriage.

That is until I met him, the person who showed me what it felt like to be wanted and appreciated.

They say when it comes to love, age is nothing but a number, and I was about to find out just how true that saying was.

The following details are how I met my King. My Jamaican King, to be exact.

Samantha

I smiled for the flashing lights of the camera. My husband's arms wrapped lovingly around me.

We were in attendance at one of the many charity functions we always attended. After all, being married to one of the most loved and respected councillors in your community gives you such perks.

"Councillor Daniel, what are your plans for the project you're working on currently? How long do you think it would take to complete?" one of the members of the press asked, as he pushed his phone to record the answer.

I turned to my husband, Councillor Adam Daniel, and halfway listened to his response. I became lost in his looks because he looked absolutely breath-taking.

He wore a black suit by Armani, and his deep dimples on his cheeks always showed, even if his face was still. He had a striking resemblance to the actor Lamann Rucker. You know, dude from the movie *Why Did I Get Married?* The one who helped Jill Scott get her sexy back; yeah, that fine brother.

Adam's build was similar to his also, nice, big, broad shoulders you would love running your nails across when he gave you the business. Hmmm, I smiled at the thought; hoping that's exactly what I would get after we left the after party we were about to attend.

"OK, that'll be all the questions for tonight. My wife and I are about to head upstairs to the after party," he said, as he hugged me even closer to him.

As usual I played my part of looking good for the cameras and keeping my ass quiet as he led me into the building. We were about to go mingle with the local rich folks in our district.

Entering the building away from the press and cameras, my husband broke our hug, and instead, he held my hand as we walked to the elevator door.

We stood in silence waiting for the doors to open. Once they did we stepped inside, and the show was over.

Adam stood to one end inside of the elevator and I stood at the other end. His face showed little to no emotion as we made our way to the top floor.

"I'm about to roll up in the after party alone. I'll tell them you suddenly fell ill. The limo will be waiting on you downstairs; you are to go out the back not the front. I'll see you in the morning."

I grinded my jaw as I listened to him. I really wanted to attend this get-together tonight. I looked down at my expensive Gucci gown; it was a shimmery silver, thin-strapped number that hugged every curve of my body. I wore the dress with a pair of Gucci heels that were covered by the length of my gown.

My shoulder length hair was styled in an up-do and my cinnamon-brown complexioned face wore very little make-up, just the way my husband liked it.

"So who is it tonight? Is it the blonde with the big, fake tits and butt injections? Or do you have a taste for Asian tonight, is it going to be Lola? You are so fucking disrespectful," I said with disgust as I shook my head; refusing to even look his way.

This was nothing new; our marriage was a big joke, a sham, an act just for the cameras and press. Happily married was a thing I couldn't even describe being married to Adam for the past four years.

My husband basically married me for appearances only; too bad he didn't bother passing the memo on to me.

He married me just to show the masses that he was supposedly happily married to a black Queen. But that was just a big fucking joke; my husband loved fucking escorts.

And not just regular escorts, he loved fucking white women and he would occasionally switch it up and have him some Asian or Chinese pussy.

"You lucky there's cameras in this elevator or I would slap the shit out you Samantha." Oh yeah, and he's a hitter. Councilman Adam Daniel loved fucking white escorts and when his wife got out of hand, as he called it, he smacked her around a little.

Not even bothering to reply, I looked at the steel elevator doors as they opened. Adam stepped out and calmly walked away, leaving me alone. I pressed the ground floor button and exhaled softly as the doors closed.

Was I about to cry or pout about my situation? Nope, I'd cried until my eyes looked like the eyes of the Asians he enjoyed fucking, on more than one occasion. I was in no mood to cry tonight, I just wanted to go home and lay in bed and catch up on my *Empire* episodes.

The doors to the elevator opened and I stepped out, making my way to the back of the building as I was told to do. Our limo driver Joseph Rock would keep me engaged in a nice conversation until I got home.

With my clutch in hand I walked out the back door without being seen. The white stretch limo awaited me, but only thing was I didn't see Joseph anywhere.

I stopped at the back door and bent and peeped in to see if he might have fallen asleep inside. Usually he would be standing at the back door waiting for me, so he could open the door for me to get in.

Suddenly, a strong, pungent smell hit me...was that weed?

I spun around and saw a figure in the distance throwing his blunt to the floor and stomping on it. I narrowed my eyes as the figure walked my way.

This definitely wasn't Joseph, but he sure was dressed in similar attire to what Joseph wore. Black pants, white shirt, and a pair of black dress shoes on his feet.

He walked up to me and raped me with eyes...twice!

"Mrs. Daniel, I'll be your driver for tonight. My name is Kingsale Rock." He held his hand out to me and I just stared at it. His voice had an accent to it that I couldn't quite make out, sounded like he was from the islands.

"Um, where is Joseph?" I asked rudely, because there was no fucking way I was about to hop in a limo with this underaged fool, who was just smoking weed.

"My uncle, I mean Joseph, had an emergency he had to deal with and left. He called me to be his replacement," he said, eventually pulling his hand back seeing that I wasn't about to shake it. He stuffed it in his pocket instead.

My eyes ran over Kingsale; he was about 6' even, light-skinned with nice brown eyes. He was a little on the slim side and his hair was low and nicely tapered down. His face was hair free and he had a pair of big, pink lips. He looked like he could be no older than twenty years old.

"You know where you're taking me to right? I won't have to direct you?" I asked, as I walked closer to the back door. I stood and waited for him to open the door for me, but I would have been standing there all damn night. Because he turned and walked off.

"Yeah I know where you live at," he said, as he spoke over his shoulder.

Shaking my head because Joseph would definitely be hearing from me about this, I opened the door and hopped in the back.

My mind wandered off to my good for nothing, cheating ass husband, as Kingsale pulled the car out. I grew the courage to ask Adam for a divorce about a month ago. But he told me I was stuck with him... "Till death do us part, remember?" was his response to me.

I felt trapped. I was in a loveless marriage all because my husband wanted to have this perfect image for the public.

My thoughts were interrupted by Reggae music and singing. I looked up and Kingsale's head bobbed back and forth. As he sang along to the song that played, his accent sounded even heavier. I think it was Bob Marley's "Redemption Song" he was singing along to.

FALLIN' FOR A JAMAICAN KING

"Excuse me, what do you think you're doing?" I asked causing him to get quiet.

"Oh my bad, Bob Marley is my nigga." My eyebrows shot up in disbelief. Why did he think it was OK to speak to me like this? I was about to put him in his place because he clearly didn't know where it was, when my phone began ringing in my clutch.

I opened the clutch and grabbed my phone, and it was my husband calling me.

"Can you please lower that?" I said to Kingsale as I answered the phone.

"Yes Adam," I said. I was secretly hoping that he somehow changed his mind and was calling to tell me to return to the after party.

"I just wanted to call and tell you that I won't be back until Monday. I'll be gone all weekend." Adam said that shit as if he called to say we were out of sugar and I needed to pick up a bag on my way home.

"Adam, what the hell, where are you going? Are you serious right now? You prefer to leave your wife alone all weekend long rather than come home to me." I know earlier I said I wasn't about to cry, but damn that. I felt the water works coming on. He had never done this before. So whoever this bitch was, was something special.

"Do you think I need your approval Samantha? I said what I said. Oh yeah, and Joseph called earlier and said he's sending a replacement driver." Those were my husband's last words before he hung up the phone on me.

Blinded by my tears, I opened the clutch and placed my phone inside. I hurriedly wiped the tears away, giving myself a pep talk to stop being a punk.

I looked up and Kingsale was staring at me from his rear-view mirror and I rolled my eyes at him.

"Can you keep your eyes on the road please?" I said with a bit of attitude because he was riding my last nerve.

"If I had an Empress as fine as you, I wouldn't let you out of my sight." To say I was shocked was an understatement. Here was this twelve-year-old, telling me, a thirty-two-year-old, grown ass woman, that she was fine. The audacity!

"Boy, please keep your eyes on the road," I said once more and looked away from him.

"I know what you're thinking, what does this twenty-nine-year-old possibly know what to do with a grown woman like yourself." I looked over at him again. So he was twenty-nine; he didn't look a day over twenty-one.

His eyes were on mine as he kept looking back at me from his rear-view mirror. He wore a big smile on his face.

"My mama believes I'm an old soul; she says she's positive I've been here before. I mean, what nigga you know that's my age listens to Barry White, Marvin Gaye and The Temptations and shit like that?" I raised my eyebrows at him because his vocabulary was horrendous.

"Oh my bad, I got carried away a little; using nigga and cuss words." He smiled at me again and I felt the corners of my mouth lifting a bit and I smiled back.

"Aw shit, is that a smile I see? Ladies and gentlemen, she smiles." Grinning broadly, I felt like a teenager who was talking to her crush and turned my head away from him, because I began feeling silly.

"Do you have any kids Mrs. Daniel?" he asked. I knew I should have reprimanded him and let him know he had no rights talking to me, furthermore even asking me my business. Somehow, I felt comfortable with him just like I did with his uncle.

"No, I don't have any kids," I said, confiding in him something that I wished I could have answered differently to. I wanted kids so badly but it never happened. I secretly went to the doctor to see if anything was wrong with me but I was given a clean bill of health. The doctor told me to just keep trying.

Unfortunately, the way Adam's and my relationship was set up, we barely had sex seeing as he was too busy fucking prostitutes of different races.

"So you just about to go home and sit by yourself all weekend long?" The least he could have done was acted like he didn't hear my conversation earlier.

"It seems that way." I looked his way again, and he was staring at me in a way that caused the insides of my stomach to flutter. What the hell was happening to me? I summed it up to lack of attention from men, preferably my husband, and the fact that I hadn't had sex in about three months.

"Can I ask where you're from? I detect an accent in your voice," I finally decided to ask him because I couldn't quite figure it out.

"Oh, I'm just a little Jamaican *bwoy*, who came to live in the U.S. with my sister when I was fourteen years old." He smiled at me as he made his accent sound even stronger answering my question.

Got me wondering if all Jamaican men were as fine as he was.

"Do you wanna go to a house party with me?" My eyes grew wide with shock at his request. This young man had definitely lost his whole mind.

"Are you crazy? Look, I shouldn't even be talking to you the way I've been, so let's just end the conversation now, OK," I told him with finality, giving him a stern look before turning my head away.

"I'm saying Mrs. Daniel, I don't think you should be alone all weekend. The least I could do is invite you to enjoy the rest of your Friday night." I cut my eyes at him, and this time he was biting into his lower lip in the most seductive way as he waited on my answer.

"Don't you have a girlfriend that you could take along with you?" I asked. Maybe it was my turn to get up in his business.

"Na, I'm too busy making this money to be tied down to a female. Besides, females my age are shifty as fuck. They be playing games like a motherfucker. Oh, my bad with all the cuss words." I brushed off the use of his profanity. I used some myself; just in my head and not out loud.

"Where is this party anyway? Not like I'm going or anything, I'm just curious to know." I already knew that he was talking about a side of town that I had no business being in. Joseph told me where he was from and it was a bad part of town. I'm pretty sure Kingsale's location would be the same.

"It's where you would refer to as the hood," he said, while snickering.

"Um, no thanks but I appreciate the invite." I felt my phone vibrate in my clutch and I took it out. It was a text message from my sister Selah, wanting to know how the after party was going.

Not being able to have the strength to tell her that Adam sent my ass home, I shoved the phone back inside of my clutch. I'd deal with her later on.

"I think you should at least give it some thought. You'll be safe with me if that's what you're worried about. No one fucks with King." It was something about the way he said that, I actually believed him.

I looked down at what I was wearing. I mean for arguments sake, if I was to attend this house party I couldn't go dressed like this. I knew for a fact I wouldn't be able to fit in; this was a two-thousand-dollar dress!

"I couldn't go dressed like this anyway," I said to him as I ran my hands down my lap of my dress.

"Don't even worry about that. My sister, she got a shit load of new shit she never wore. We'll just stop by her place and she'll hook you up. So it's settled; you about to attend a house party in the hood." I began shaking my head at him because I said no fucking thing.

"Um, I never said that. Please, just take me home."

"Look, we'll make a deal. If you don't enjoy the party I promise I'll take you home as soon as you ask me to. Deal?" We looked at one another from the mirror as I contemplated his proposal, biting into my lip.

Maybe I should learn to live a little. My husband was doing just that. His face was probably chin deep in some escort's funky pussy right now. Looking at Kingsale, he didn't seem like the murdering type. And he looked like he had pussy thrown his way every time he left his house, so I was sure he wasn't a rapist either.

Against my better judgement and rational thinking, I opened my mouth to reply.

"OK, I'll go," I said quietly.

Samantha

I changed my mind a total of twenty times before we pulled up to Kingsale's sister's apartment. He had called his sister beforehand and told her he was coming and what he needed from her.

I looked around nervously at my surroundings before he got out and opened my back door. *Oh, so now he opens the door,* I thought to myself as I climbed out.

Growing up in a family that was considered well-off, I knew nothing about these parts of town where gunshots would be heard often. Crack-heads could be seen looking to purchase their next hit, girls walked around half-naked, and dope boys sold their product on the corner.

"Why the fuck you look like you about to shit on yourself, Empress?" I gasped at how outspoken Kingsale was.

He snickered as he led me toward the entrance of the building. A few guys were standing to the front looking shady as hell and smiled and hollered when they saw us approaching.

"Nigga, where in the fuck you get a limo from?" a dark-skinned fella asked who had tear-drop tattoos trailing from his left eye. He looked me over as if I was standing there butt-naked.

"Uncle Joseph couldn't work tonight so I took his spot. Make sure nobody fucks with it," Kingsale said, taking a few bills from out his pocket and slapping it in the guy's hand.

"Damn, who's your friend King?" an oversized one with corn-rows asked, his eyes roaming over me boldly. He smirked and I saw he had one of his front teeth missing., Kingsale replied rudely as we made our way inside.

"Lucky for you, my sister lives on the first floor. I see you struggling in them heels Sammie." My neck twisted so that I could look over in his direction. Did I ever give him my first name?

"My uncle Joseph gave me your entire name, so don't look so shocked." He chuckled, stopping in front of a door and knocked on it as if he was law enforcement.

The door flung open violently and I jumped back.

"The fuck is wrong with you King? You can't be knocking on my door like you five-O." The female who wore a very angry scowl on her face was indeed his sister; the resemblance was uncanny. Her accent wasn't as thick as King's, almost as if she was trying to mask it. I didn't see why; that accent sounded like melody to me.

Kingsale placed his palm across her face and shoved her back, causing her to lose her balance in the process.

"The hell you think you talking to like that Kwana?" he said as he stepped inside the apartment. "Just remember I'm your older brother, respect my Jamaican gangsta."

"You older by ten minutes fool," she said, slapping his back and closing the door behind us. By ten minutes, that would mean—

"Samantha, meet my twin sister Kwana," he said, as he introduced us walking off toward her kitchen.

"Hello, it's so nice to meet you." I held out my hand to her and she shook it as she eyed my gown.

"Damnnnn, what kind of dress is this? This shit is tight girl." She fingered the material of my gown as she looked at it in fascination.

"Kwana! Stop acting country. And why you ain't have nothing to eat in this refrigerator?!" Kingsale hollered out at her as he rummaged through her fridge.

"Nigga, did you buy anything up in this bitch and put it in there? I don't think so." She rolled her eyes dramatically at him as he slammed the door of her fridge shut. I smiled as I watched the way they interacted with each other. Even though they were acting as though they couldn't stand each other, I could tell they had nothing but love for one another.

"Where my nephew at?" Kingsale asked as he walked to where we stood.

"He sleep, and don't go back there and wake him up either." He waved her off before making his way down her corridor to one of her bedrooms.

"Come on girl, let's see what I have that would look good on you," she said as she took my hand in hers and led me to a door opposite to the one Kingsale disappeared in.

Exactly twenty minutes later, I was standing in front of Kwana's full-length mirror doubting the reflection I saw was mine. Kwana dressed me in a loose fitting, black, thin-strapped, long romper.

Even though the fit was loose, all of my curves easily showed and my ass sat nice and upright in the back. She completed the look with a black, strappy sandal.

I even got a new hairstyle. She took down my up-do and my hair fell to my shoulders in loose curls.

"You popping in that outfit girl. You could go ahead and keep it when you're done." I looked over at her and couldn't possibly expect her to just give me something she never wore before. So I offered to pay her for it.

"Don't be silly, you're my brother's girl, right? Don't even sweat it." I started to correct her assumption of my relationship with her brother, when he suddenly stepped inside of the room.

He was also wearing new attire, and I couldn't keep my eyes off him. He wore a pair of grey sweat pants, a plain white T-shirt, and a pair of what I believed to be Jordan's on his feet.

Kingsale's arms were littered with tattoos of all sizes and colors. They were hidden before because of the long-sleeved shirt he was wearing. He wore a gold chain with an iced-out pendant that read the word "King" on it. The chain hung from his neck and it reached mid-way on his stomach.

My pussy began to react in a way that it shouldn't for someone that was three years my junior.

In Kingsale's hand, however, was the cutest little baby boy I'd ever seen. He could have been no more than some months old. He was light-skinned like his mother and uncle, with a pair of light-pink lips, and he was staring at me with a pair of light-brown eyes as if we'd met before.

"Say hello to Kaden, my nephew," Kingsale said as he stared at the baby with nothing but adoration.

"Didn't I say not to wake him?" Kwana fussed at her brother as she went to take her son from out his arms. But Kingsale turned away from her so the baby remained in his arms.

"Take yo' time Kwana. He was up when I walked in the room." Kingsale walked up to me and held Kaden out so I could take him.

"You wanna hold him? Seems as if you got baby fever in your eyes." I smiled up at him and took the baby from out of his reach. I fell in love at that very moment when Kaden held on to me, as he looked up at me in curiosity. Probably wondering who the hell was holding him.

He cooed softly as I rocked him gently. Not being able to resist I played with the little curls at the top of his head.

"I need to use your car right quick Kwana," Kingsale said to his sister.

"Get the fuck outta here King. Where is your ride?" Kwana came up to me, gently removing her son from my arms.

"I rolled up here in a limo. I took Uncle Joseph's shift tonight since something came up with him. I can't go to Tek's party in a limo, so come on and give me your keys. I'll bring it back later." Sucking her teeth loudly at her brother, she walked out the bedroom with Kingsale and myself trailing behind her.

Picking her keys up from a small table at the centre of her living room, she handed them to Kingsale.

"We 'bout to bounce, I'll see you later. Bye Kaden," Kingsale said, bending as he kissed his nephew repeatedly.

Turning to me, he grabbed my hand and led us to the front door.

"Thanks for everything Kwana," I said, breaking free from Kingsale's hold so that I could give her a quick hug. I caressed Kaden's cheek gently and he smiled at me causing my heart to melt.

As we left his sister's apartment he took my hand again and pulled me closer to him so he could whisper in my ear.

"You look fucking sweet by the way." My heart began thumping loudly in my chest as I looked up at him. And he watched me in return with want.

Walking outside, the same group of guys were standing outside talking loudly. When they saw us coming they all got quiet and gawked at me. They were probably thinking Kingsale walked in with one chick and walked out with another.

Leading me to his sister's Kia Sorento, he opened the door for me and allowed me to hop in. Before closing my door, he said, "Let me go handle something with my niggas and I'll be back." Not giving me time to reply, he jogged off in the direction where the crew of fellas were standing.

Out of curiosity, I watched as he spoke to the guy with the gap in his mouth. I narrowed my eyes as Kingsale held out his hand and the gap-toothed guy handed him what looked like a ziplocked bag filled with something.

Now I was no expert, but I was almost certain Kingsale just took a bag full of some sort of drug. I turned to the front as he climbed in the vehicle, with whatever he just purchased tucked away in his pocket.

"You ready?" he asked me with a broad grin on his face.

"I guess so," I replied as he pulled off. I was on my way to my first house party in a part of town I'd never been before.

❦

TO MY PLEASANT SURPRISE, the party was a lot of fun. Everyone was friendly, and most importantly, nobody knew who I was.

I learned the house party was really a birthday party for his friend named Tek, who would be turning twenty the following day. I was partying with a bunch of kindergarteners!

Tek obviously got his nickname because of the many tattoos he had of the gun all over his arms.

I also realized that what King got from his friend...I was calling him King now 'cause he told me to. He was selling some type of drugs; the people in attendance kept approaching him. He would then dip in his pocket after they spoke in his ear and a quick exchange would be made.

I questioned him about it, but he told me it was nothing I should be worried about.

We had been here for almost two, maybe three hours. I was on my fifth glass of a drink called Ace of Spades, and it was safe to say I was beginning to get drunk. I was enjoying myself so much that not one time did the thought of my husband cross my mind.

There were a few girls in attendance who kept trying really hard to get King's attention, but their efforts went un-noticed by him. And I must admit, he'd been nothing but a perfect gentleman to me all night.

He kept his hands to himself and made sure I wasn't needing of anything. He even accompanied me when I needed to use the bathroom. Which, by the way, I needed to use right now.

I tugged on his arm as he bobbed his head to another one of the many songs I didn't know.

"I need to use the bathroom again," I said, while doing a little dance on the spot so he knew I couldn't hold it.

"Damn Sammie, again?" he asked as I smiled, loving the nickname he had given me. Only my sister called me Sammie.

"Come on." He grabbed my hand and led me down a narrow, dark corridor that was overflowing with a bunch of horny twenty-some-thing year olds feeling up on each other.

I waited a couple of minutes being third in the pee-line, eagerly running in when it was my turn. I stripped out of the romper and relieved myself. Rompers were cute and all, until it was time to pee and you had to get practically naked.

I washed my hands, taking a look at myself in the mirror. I almost screamed at the reflection that looked back at me.

My eyes were bloodshot red, barely able to stay open on their own. I needed to lie down for a quick minute.

I walked out of the bathroom, stumbling in the process. King rushed to grab me before I fell over.

"I think I'm drunk," I said to him as I smiled like a demented person. King looked at me, and his expression changed to one of concern...I think.

"Maybe I should get you home," he said, as he held on to my hand as we made our way down the crowded corridor.

As we passed a closed door, I reached for the knob and turned it and was relieved when it opened. I pulled out of King's hand and stepped inside; it was a bedroom.

"Aye, what the fuck Sammie? Come on, let me get yo' drunk ass home." Ignoring his words, I walked over to the bed and dropped down on it with a loud thud.

I closed my eyes as I listened to the sound of the bedroom door being closed. I felt the shift of the mattress, letting me know that King had taken a seat next to me.

"Mmmmm," I groaned softly as I felt the room start to spin.

"You probably shouldn't lie down. You may need to vomit." Oh, was that what was happening to me?

I sat up in the bed and looked over at King who was staring at me, and I smiled at him.

He just sat there with a weird expression on his face.

"You're so beautiful, you know that? Your husband don't fucking deserve you; he's a *batty boy*." I swear those words sobered me up a little. First off, I had no fucking idea what a *batty boy* was. And secondly, within the past few hours I'd been with King, he made me feel more appreciated and wanted in the four years I'd been married.

I was about to say something to him, when I heard a familiar song begin playing from the party going on outside.

I stood up and pulled King by his hand, begging him to dance with me.

"What! This is my jam...what!" I shrieked in excitement as King looked at me with an amused look on his face. He stood up and I walked over to the closed door so that I could rest my back on it for support.

I didn't trust myself to not topple over.

Tell me what kind of man, would treat his woman so cold,

Treat you like you're nothing, when you're worth more than gold.

Joe's sweet voice came through the door, as I sang along to the words of "All The Things." I reached up and wrapped my arms around King's neck as we swayed to the music.

I tried to remember the words as I sang along. King's hand was on my hips as I pulled on his neck wanting to feel his body closer to mine.

"Sammie," he said, his voice so raspy it didn't sound like his anymore. I looked up at him and he looked down at me, and the mood in the room instantly changed.

King took his hand and gently ran his thumb across my lower lip, as he stared at it lustfully.

Maybe it was my inebriated state, but I wanted to feel his full, pink lips against mine.

"Sammie, what are you doing to me?" he asked. I tugged on his neck, forcing his face down to mine, and I kissed him.

When our lips touched it felt like something I'd always wanted my entire life. We hungrily entwined our tongues with each other's as I pressed my body into his.

"Stop, Sammie, are you sure you want this? Because once I start I won't be able to stop," he asked me as I tried to find his lips again, pissed that he broke our kiss.

"Yes, yes. I want this. Please King," I begged him as my eyes said exactly how I was feeling and how bad I wanted this.

He continued staring at me for a few seconds more, before he crushed his lips to mine again causing a moan from deep within me.

Pressing me hard against the door, his hand travelled down to between my legs and squeezed my pussy from the outside of my romper.

"Take this the fuck off," he growled, as he roughly tugged the straps down and removed my attire in the blink of an eye.

"Shit," he said, as he looked at me clad in my bra and underwear. He hissed as he cupped my breasts, un-clasping the front hook and throwing the material at our feet.

I closed my eyes as he dipped his head, taking a hardened nipple between his lips. He suckled me, flicking his tongue back and forth against my nipple.

I pushed forward, grabbing the back of his head wanting to feel more of him. As he moved his mouth over to my other nipple, his hand travelled to the front of my panties.

I cried out when his fingers aggressively rubbed me through the fabric. I enjoyed every single erotic touch his hand and his mouth were doing to my body.

"King," I groaned as he ripped my underwear off and dipped his finger inside of my wetness.

"Oh shit, this fucking pussy gushing, Sammie." Looking up at me, he held my gaze as his fingers attacked my insides. His index and middle finger assaulted my walls and his thumb circled my clit.

"You like that?" he said as he stood upright, his free hand flat against the door as he pressed his body into mine. His face mere inches from mine as he breathed into my face.

My mouth formed an O, as I nodded in reply.

"You about to give a young King this juicy *punanny*?" he asked, as he bent his head and began sucking on my neck. His fingers slowed down as he began to suck on my earlobe.

Jesus Christ! How was a twenty-nine-year-old able to make me feel this way?

"Yes...yes," I managed to say to him. Removing his hand from my wetness, he wrapped it around my neck and spoke in my ear.

"Get your ass over there and lay on the bed. Let this Jamaican rude boy do things to you I know your husband never did." His breath tickled my face as his lips were pressed on my ear.

With knees that buckled with every shaky step I took, I laid down on the bed. I watched as King made his way over to me, pulling his T-shirt over his head. I curled my lips in as I looked at his wonderful, half-naked body.

Expecting to see the remainder of his upper body with the same drawings he had on his arms, I was left in surprise as his chest and abdominals were tattoo free.

Pulling his chain over his head, he placed it on a dresser behind him. He tugged on his grey sweat pants and lowered it, so that it rested low on his hip.

Giving me full view of his V disappearing inside of his pants.

Standing before me, he signalled me to come to him by wiggling his index finger.

"Come to the end of the bed," he instructed me. With shaky breaths, I inched my butt to the edge and King wasted no time to get on his knees between my thighs.

Kissing tenderly on my inner thighs, he flicked his tongue like he was a cross-breed between human and snake. I looked down at the top of his head as he slowly made his way to my throbbing, aching pussy.

I once heard a rumour that Jamaican men didn't eat pussy, but King was about to prove that rumour to be bullshit.

With his hands placed under the back of my thighs, he suddenly lifted my legs forcing me to lay back on the bed.

And then his mouth was on me. With just the tip of his tongue, he ran it in one quick movement from the end of my slit straight to my pulsing clit.

I tried to run away from the intense pleasure that motion alone gave me. But he held me in place, shoving my legs further upward to my chest. King dived in tongue first eating me out as if it was the best thing he'd ever tasted.

It was the sloppiest head I'd ever gotten! He intentionally allowed his saliva to run out of his mouth adding to my wetness, only to slurp it up again; then to empty his saliva into my slit all over again.

His tongue-tip circled my clit, over and over again, and I moaned in ecstasy as I grinded my wetness in his face.

"Shit!" I hollered out, as he inserted two fingers in me while he sucked on my clit, humming loudly as he did so.

"Buss in my mouth, Sammie," he said, as I looked down at him and he looked up at me with his mouth full of my pussy.

The way he was staring at me was so sexy as he sucked on my clit. I placed my hand at the back of his head, raising my ass as I felt my orgasm creeping up on me.

"Mmmmm," he groaned, as I felt my wetness seeping out of me as I shook with my first orgasm. Not bothering to let go of my clit, he kept up his assault as I tried to escape him yet again. I dragged my ass up on the bed as I ran from his tongue.

King refused to let me go as he followed my retreat, never letting go of my clit. I felt another orgasm coming on and I froze, shutting my eyes tightly.

"Uh...uh...uh," I gasped loudly. Thank god for the loud music being played, or I would have alerted the party-goers of what was taking place in this bedroom.

Grabbing the sheets, I bunched them up in my hands as my body writhed in pleasure as I came even harder than the first time.

Standing to his feet, King held my waist and dragged me down once more to the edge of the bed. Shoving his hand inside of his pants pocket, he pulled out a foil wrapper and ripped it open with his teeth.

Still trying to come down from my orgasmic high, I watched in silence as King dropped his sweatpants and boxers around his ankles. My eyes couldn't look away at the wonderful sight of his big, meaty dick.

He licked his lips as he rolled the condom over his erection.

"I'mma 'bout to beat this *punanny* up," he said to me as he held his dick in hand. He opened his mouth and allowed a mouthful of saliva to drop from his mouth to his dick. Using his hand, he rubbed the saliva across his rubber encased dick.

Since the bed was high enough, he was almost levelled with my pussy so he was able to remain in a standing position as he placed his dick at my opening.

I looked down between us as he used the head of his dick to smear my wetness around on my slit. I sucked in my breath as he distributed the wetness on my clit, stopping to tap his dick head against my aching nub.

With one hand on my waist holding me in position, he entered me aggressively. His length and girth stretching me like I'd never been stretched before.

Shit! I screamed repeatedly in my head because my mouth just couldn't form the word. My body rocked violently as King punished my insides, only I had no idea for what.

As I looked into his face, his eyes were closed, his lower lip tucked inside his mouth and his face wore a sinister expression, as he brutally dealt with my pussy that had never, ever been treated this way before.

"Fuckkkkkk," he released a throaty groan as he removed himself from me. He replaced his dick with his tongue, but not in my pussy this time, in my back exit. I tried to run again, but just like the first time he held me in place.

"Please King," I begged him, realizing that I couldn't take any more. His tongue played with my anus as his fingers rubbed on my clit.

"Please King, what?" he asked me as he stood up again, his dick in his hand. "Didn't you tell me I could have this pussy?" he asked, as he placed himself at my opening again.

He shoved it inside me, grabbing me by surprise, but he exited me just as fast as he entered me.

"Answer me Sammie, didn't you say I could have this juicy *punanny?*" He slammed into me once more, but this time I anticipated it.

"Yessssssss," I hissed, as he continued his punishment. He remained deep inside of me, rotating his hips so that I felt every inch of him.

"I want you to remember this night as long as you live." *Who in the fuck told him I was about to forget!* I thought as he rammed inside of me. I felt my skin begin to tear as he forced my legs open even wider.

For the next twenty minutes King savagely fucked me. At one time, I swore I would pass out.

He began to choke me as his hand closed around my throat, as he hit every spot, deep in my core.

His pace quickened at last letting me know our tryst was about to come to an end.

"Shit...shit...shit," he groaned, tilting his head back as he reached up to grab my breasts. His body twitched into an epileptic orgasm and he dropped his body on mine.

I wrapped my arms around him as the thought that I just cheated on my husband with a twenty-nine-year-old left me feeling slightly ashamed.

King raised his head and looked deeply into my eyes, as if he wanted to say something, but changed his mind; he kissed me instead.

Laying his head back onto my chest, no words were spoken as we knew to ourselves, that this would be the last time we would probably see each other.

Samantha

Two years later...

"Damn Sammie, it smells good in here," my sister, Selah, said as she walked inside of my kitchen.

I smiled as she approached to give me a kiss, our usual way of greeting each other.

"I didn't even hear you come in," I said to her as I grabbed a plate to dish out a serving of the breakfast I prepared for myself and Adam.

"I still have a key remember," she said, as she shook the key in my face. I rolled my eyes forgetting completely I gave her a key a while back.

Taking the plate, I handed it to her with pancakes, eggs and bacon. She made her way over to the island in the middle of my very spacious kitchen as she sat down.

"Where's your loser husband at?" she asked, as she stuffed a forkful of eggs, bacon and pancakes inside of her mouth.

"Where's your ex-con man at?" Adam replied, as he walked into the kitchen, hearing Selah's description of him.

Stepping to me, he placed a quick kiss on my cheek as I handed him his morning coffee.

"Shut up, I can't wait for my sister to finally come to her senses and divorce your ass." She sneered her lips up at him as she spoke.

Making my own plate, I remained silent as I sat next to my sister, not even bothering to comment on her and Adam's usual argument.

They didn't like each other and made it no secret.

"After six years of marriage, she ain't about to go nowhere. When you gonna get that?" He made his way out of the kitchen as he prepared to leave for the day, not even bothering to say good-bye to me.

We waited for the front door to close before we could begin to talk in comfort.

"I wish you'd leave him already and find you a good nigga," Selah said, which she always did.

Not even bothering to waste my time to answer her, I ate in silence as I picked the morning paper from off the granite counter-top and opened it up.

"How is Lamar?" I asked her as I began flipping through the pages of the newspaper with little interest.

"Ugh, don't get me started on that nigga." Now, even though my sister and I grew up in a safe neighbourhood with parents who had great jobs, my mother being a child psychologist and my daddy being a college professor, we had been sheltered from the cruel world.

But my sister, she always found a way to disobey our parents. She cut school, smoked weed, and managed to get involved with just about every bad boy in our district that we grew up in.

Her current boyfriend Lamar was no different from all the rest of the low-life brothers that she dealt with.

I listened with feigned interest as she explained the fiasco of a relationship she was going through.

As I flipped through the newspapers and landed on the third page, my heart skipped a series of beats as a familiar face was plastered big and bold on the page.

Kingsale Rock, released from prison, the headline read. I placed my fork on my plate quietly as I read the story.

Kingsale Rock, who was charged two years prior for drug possession, has been released a year early. Mr. Rock was held with a bag full of ecstasy pills and Molly with the purpose to sell two years ago. Kingsale was released when his lawyer requested that he needed to attend the funeral of his mother on the grounds of good behaviour.

When asked how he felt about his early release Mr. Rock replied, that he was happy to be able to attend the funeral service of his mother and to be reunited with his twin sister and nephew.

I read in silence as Selah continued ranting on about her man.

I hadn't seen King since that night I gave my body to him in ways I'd never even given to my husband. After we left the party and he dropped me home, I learned the next morning, via the news, that he was stopped in a routine road block and after being searched, the officers found the drugs he had purchased earlier that night in his pocket.

I was crushed beyond belief, far more than anyone could imagine. I wanted to visit him on many occasions, wanted to write him to let him know that I thought about him every single day.

I never did any of those things, but I stayed in agony for the last two years thinking of him. He would be thirty-one years of age now and I remembered every detail of that night.

"Are you listening to me?" Selah asked, as she brought me out of my reverie.

"Anyways, hurry up and get dressed. Let's go hit up the mall and spend your husband's money, girl!" she shrieked as she threw both her hands up in the air in excitement. All I could do was laugh as I got up from around the island.

Placing our dishes in the sink, I turned to her as I made my way out of the kitchen to shower and get dressed.

"Get to washing the dishes while I get ready, Selah," I said to her as I heard her suck her teeth.

"Tell that cheap husband of yours to get a fucking maid," she barked at me as I walked out the kitchen to make my way up the stairs.

After my shower I stood in my walk-in closet and flipped through an array of clothing, wondering what to wear.

My eyes fell on a shoe box and I smiled a distant smile. Bending down, I opened the box and took out the left side of the red bottom Louis Vuitton heels. Turning it upside down, the oversized gold chain fell into the palm of my hand.

The words on the pendant read "King," and I passed the tips of my fingers across each letter.

That night, we explored every inch of each other's bodies a total of three times. When we were done and were getting dressed, King came up behind me and placed the chain around my neck.

I remembered turning around to look at him confused and he gently touched my cheek.

"Hold on to this for me. When you think you're ready to see me again, call me, and I'll come anywhere you at and get it from you."

I smiled before tucking it back in the inside of my shoes. Placing the shoe back in the box, I replaced the lid.

I continued looking for something to wear, finally deciding on a pair of denim shorts and a denim shirt with black Converse on my feet.

I looked at myself in the mirror and sighed at my weight gain. I gained weight after I stopped going to the gym on a regular, the extra pounds settling on my hips and ass.

Adam strongly disapproved of my new figure, but I paid him no mind. He could stay fucking his plastic Barbies for all I cared. I ran my fingers through my now shorter hair; I sported a layered bob, honey blonde in color.

Nodding my head in approval, I walked off and made my way to meet my sister.

"Selah, we've been walking this mall for an hour now. Would you please hurry up and pick a gift already?" I whined as we walked out of like the tenth store.

Selah's boyfriend's birthday was coming up and she was looking for a gift for him. I told her his ass didn't deserve shit, but she didn't listen to me.

"Ok, I'll just get the pair of old school Jordan's we saw in Shoelocker. I sucked my teeth because Shoelocker was about five stores down.

"Bitch, I told you to get it while we were in there," I grumbled at her, and she gasped at me in shock.

"Well look who turned hood all of a sudden. Just throwing the word bitch around." She snickered at me. Holding her hand, I dragged her in the direction of the store, ignoring what she said.

While in the store I examined a pair of Nike sneakers that were on the shelf and was kind of shocked at how much people spent on these things.

Selah waited for one of the clerks to check on the size she requested as I inspected the overly priced shoes.

"You traded your Gucci heels for Nike's?" a familiar voice, with a slight accent, said to the back of me. I froze with the pair of Air Force One's in my hand.

I turned around slowly and a pair of light-brown eyes were looking back at me.

I almost melted right there on the spot as I looked in the face of King. I did nothing for the next couple of minutes but stare at him. He looked so different; the picture they had of him in the newspapers clearly was an old one.

King was now sporting a well-maintained beard, and it highlighted his full, pink lips even more. He still wore his hair in a low cut. My eyes travelled down his body at what looked like weight gain, but with only muscles.

His arms looked bigger and well-toned, his tattoos glistened against his skin. His chest stuck out a little, obviously showing that he'd been lifting weights.

His Gucci sweat pants and short-sleeved T-shirt hugged his new and improved body. I wanted nothing more than to pull him into my arms and hug him tightly. But the stone-cold expression he wore told me I should probably just turn and make a run for it.

"King," I finally was able to say to him. He held on to a few shopping bags in his hand as he continued to stare at me.

"Mrs. Daniel," he said, almost in a sarcastic tone.

"Um, I-I," I stuttered out, lost for words, feeling embarrassed that I wasn't even able to form a proper sentence.

King had a slight smirk on his face. But his eyes were hard and almost expressionless, and I felt as though he wasn't as happy to see me as I was happy to see him.

"It's so nice to see you," I said, feeling proud of myself that I remembered how to make a complete sentence.

"Thanks," he replied dryly as he looked over my shoulder.

"Sammie, I didn't know you knew King," Selah said as she came and stood next to us. "How do you know my baby sister, King?"

"Hey, Selah, let yo' nigga, Lamar, know I'm having a get-together over at Kwana's place. You welcome to swing by and bring someone along if you wish." After saying the last part, he looked at me briefly, making me swallow nervously. "I'll let your sister tell you how we met."

"Sure, I'll let him know. It's good to see you again," Selah said.

Giving Selah a smile and a head nod, he turned to me and said, "I'll see you around Mrs. Daniel." He walked off and my eyes followed him as he stopped and talked to a girl that was also shopping in the store. I felt a pang of jealously as he took her hand in his and they walked out, just as he placed his hand around her shoulders hugging her closer to him.

"Little prim and proper Samantha knows the big, bad, infamous, Kingsale Rock." I waved her off as we made our way out of the store.

"So you gonna tell me how you know him or what?" she continued to pry.

I gave her a half-ass story of him replacing Joseph one night when Joseph couldn't make it for work and left it at that.

She side-eyed me as if she didn't believe my story, but I refused to say any more.

"Well, since you know him I guess you can tag along with Lamar and I to his sister's, for his little get-together." I gawked at her as if she had gone completely mad.

There was no way in hell I was about to end up in the same room with King again!

Hell would have to freeze over!

Kingsale

"Come here Kaden." I ran behind my little nephew as he tried to get away from me. I laughed as he shrieked out with excitement as I grabbed him up and lifted him up on my shoulders.

"The hell is you doing, King? Take care you throw him down," Kwana fussed at me as I held my nephew high in the air.

Ignoring her, I continued walking around her apartment with Kaden on my shoulders.

I was the happiest nigga around. I was a free man again and I planned on spending a lot of time with my twin sister and my nephew.

I missed out on a whole two years of Kaden's life. The little nigga had no idea who the fuck I was when he saw me. That shit broke my fucking heart.

I walked over to a photo of our mother my sister had of her hanging on the wall.

"Look Kaden, it's grandma," I said as I stared lovingly at her smiling face. I was going to miss my mother so much. Shit was hard enough that I wasn't around in her final years.

She had diabetes and ended up getting complications and passed away a few weeks ago. It was only because she passed that I was out;

FALLIN' FOR A JAMAICAN KING

that and I'd been on my best behaviour on the inside. A nigga did his best to stay the fuck out of trouble while I was locked up.

The night I got locked up after having the best sex a nigga had in years, I had forgotten all about having the drugs on me. I took Samantha back to my sister's, so I could pick up the limo, and after dropping Samantha off at her house I came up on a roadblock.

Of course a nigga driving a limo was unheard of to the white cops that stopped me, so they immediately pulled my black ass over. They found a Ziplock bag filled with Molly, Percocet, weed and Ecstasy pills.

It's not like a nigga never got locked up before; I was the biggest distributor of weed around where I lived. I got the best Jamaican grade of weed, and motherfuckers came far and wide to purchase my shit.

That night I took those pills on a whim; I'd never sold fucking pills before. But I knew when people were partying, getting turnt and shit, they did any type of drugs that were available.

I walked over to Kwana and handed Kaden over to her.

"Don't forget you buying the alcohol for your welcome home party. I'm not even about to supply that shit for your crew, a bitch would go broke," Kwana said as she went to the refrigerator and handed Kaden a juice box.

"Don't sweat it, I got it," I said, walking over to her sofa and sitting down. My mind went back to running into Samantha earlier at the mall.

Just the thought of her caused my dick to twitch in my sweats. She had put on some weight in all the right places, and she wore her hair a little differently. She was looking so fucking good I wanted to grab her hand and drag her ass inside one of the changing rooms, so that I could fuck the shit out of her.

Unknown to her, I spotted her about ten minutes before I decided to go up and talk to her. I saw her and her sister shopping and I followed them. A nigga done turned into a stalker. I never in my fucking life followed a chick before as if I was a fucking puppy.

That shit was fucked up, but I didn't care. I did it anyway.

When I saw Samantha standing alone holding a pair of sneakers in her hand, it was like my feet had a mind of their own. I walked over to her with all intentions of wrapping my arms around her.

That plan came to an abrupt halt as I approached her only to realize that she was still wearing her wedding band.

Why in the actual fuck was she still married to that *batty boy*? Instead of giving her the greeting that I had wanted to, I ended up being all up in my feelings.

It was beyond me why she was still married to someone who obviously didn't give two fucks about her. Samantha must have really loved being unhappy.

"What you over there thinking?" Kwana said as she sat next to me with Kaden in her lap, sucking away on the straw of his juice box.

I reached over and plucked his big toe and he snickered at me.

"Guess who I saw before I came over here," I said to her as she shrugged her shoulders at me.

"Remember Samantha Daniel?" I asked her, as she searched her brain trying to remember who I was speaking about.

"You mean Mrs. Samantha Daniel," she replied, as she stressed on the *Mrs.* for emphasis. I sucked my teeth loudly at her, dismissing what she was getting at.

"King, that night you never once mentioned who she was. I knew her ass looked slightly familiar. You still messing with the councilman's wife?" she asked, her voice getting real low as if we weren't the only ones in the room.

"Man, it wasn't even like that with her," I said, trying my best to sound unconcerned about Samantha.

"Who you fooling? I know you liked that chick way more than you're letting on." Sometimes having a twin fucking sucked; it's like she could sense shit.

"Yeah well, she's married, so whatever." I ran my fingers through my newly grown beard.

"Why don't you invite her over here on Saturday? I'm sure she'll come." I sucked my teeth at her question.

"Didn't you yourself just mention that she is married! *Boomboclat,*

Kwana." I shook my head and she reached over and pushed me by my forehead.

"Why get defensive if you don't like the bitch?" I sucked my teeth at her again.

"She was with her sister when I saw her too. I never even knew Selah and she were related." I knew of Selah through her nigga Lamar. He was a cool nigga. He loved the ladies though but then again, what nigga didn't.

"Lamar's Selah?" Kwana asked with her eyebrows raised. I nodded my head letting her know she was right.

Kwana began discussing Lamar and the many females she swore she knew for a fact he fucked. But my sister was just being her normal messy self. I halfway listened to her when there was a soft knock at her door.

I looked at her waiting for her to let me know if she was expecting company. She shrugged her shoulders, her way of saying she had no idea who it was.

I stood to my feet and put my hand at my waist to feel for my weapon, even though I knew it was there. When I got to the door I peeked out and groaned softly to myself.

"Hey, Uncle Joseph," I said as I swung the door open and walked back to the sofa to have a seat. My uncle didn't even bother to acknowledge me as he casually walked in.

Uncle Joseph was a really nice person, always doing his best to keep my ass out of trouble. He moved from Jamaica to live in the U.S. from as long as I could remember. He didn't even have an accent anymore. He encouraged my mother to move soon after, bringing Kwana and I along with her, so we all could have a better life.

However, the fast life got my ass. I ended up selling weed and being the top dog in my community. These niggas were out here selling some weak ass grade, so I introduced them to that high-grade Jamaican kush.

Right now, however, my uncle and I weren't really on speaking terms. He wasn't all that pleased when he found out two years ago I took the limo, parked it up in the hood, and got arrested afterward.

Personally, I thought he should get over it. I mean, that was two fucking years ago. But apparently, he almost lost his job since Samantha's pussyhole husband almost fired him.

"Kingsale," was all he said as he walked past me choosing to sit where my sister was seated. I shook my head at his disapproving demeanor as I slouched down in my seat.

I listened silently as they spoke about my mother's funeral service and the reading of her will. I planned on not accepting anything my mother may have left for me. I wanted everything to go to my sister and my nephew.

"Anyway, I really came over here to let you know that I would be retiring soon. I plan on returning to Jamaica by the end of the month."

Kwana and I exchanged glances but said nothing. To me, it wasn't surprising that my uncle wanted to return to our homeland. He never married and never had any kids, so returning home would make sense.

"Kingsale, I was hoping you would consider accepting my job. I was able to put in a good word for you with Mr. Daniel, and he said he would be willing to give you another chance." Kwana started coughing in a dramatic fashion and I narrowed my eyes at her.

Now my uncle had no idea about Samantha and me, and the fact that she and I were with each other a couple hours before on the same night I got arrested. I sat back and thought about this for a minute, wondering if Samantha was worth it. It didn't take me long to know the answer to that.

"What does Mrs. Daniel think about all this?" It was important that I knew if Samantha wanted me there or not. If she wasn't OK with me working for her and her husband, I would respect her wishes.

"I honestly don't think Mr. Daniel has spoken to her about it. Besides, he wouldn't need her approval; he's a kind of no-nonsense guy. What he says goes, don't matter if she's ok with it or not." I didn't know why, but hearing those words really irritated me and I wished I could meet that asshole so that I could wrap my hands around his neck. He didn't deserve to be married to her.

"It's also a good way to stay out of trouble Kingsale. Think about your mother. I don't think she'd be happy knowing that you got out of jail and you're up to your old tricks again." My uncle just had to rub that shit in; all that did was make me feel bad about myself.

"Well let me know what you decide so I could pass word on to Mr. Daniel. This is a good opportunity Kingsale. It may not be how you saw your life, but it would be good to keep your hands busy with something other than street drugs." I snorted at his words as he got up to leave.

I got up to walk him out, thinking if I really wanted to drive around a stuck-up nigga and his wife I fucked, who by the way had the best pussy a nigga ever had. I wanted to make my momma proud, even if she wasn't here physically. Plus, I needed to lay low for a while being fresh out of prison and all.

Even though I knew this was a fucked up idea and that I had no business taking this particular job, my mouth opened and replied anyway.

"I don't mind taking the job. If it would keep a nigga out of trouble." Uncle Joseph smiled as he stood outside the door.

"This would be good for you Kingsale. Only positive things would come from this and it would keep your ass off the streets. You know Samantha asked for you a few times when you were locked up." This piqued my interest and I tried to play it off subtly.

"Oh really, she did?" I shoved my hands inside of my sweatpants pocket.

"Yeah, she always wanted to know how you were doing. I think you made a really good impression with her that one night you filled in for me." I couldn't help but laugh in my head because my uncle had no idea the kind of impression he was talking about.

"Well I'm glad I did. Let's hope she's still enthusiastic when she sees I got the job as your replacement."

Samantha

I couldn't even lie; I'd been all in my feelings since the day I saw King. There wasn't a day that went by and he didn't cross my thoughts, seeing him again and how much he looked like he matured.

I knew I had no business thinking about him as much as I was, but I couldn't help it.

Today was the welcome home party for him over at his sister's place. Selah did ask me if I would accompany her when she called me last night, but I told her I couldn't.

Adam walked into our bedroom fresh out the shower and from the looks of it, he seemed as if he was about to go out somewhere.

I was still laying in bed, it was eight in the morning, and I had no clue where he was about to go this early on a Saturday morning.

"You about to go somewhere?" I asked him softly, making sure I used the correct tone when I asked the question. There were times Adam refused to answer any questions I asked him because he told me I wasn't using the right tone.

"Yes."

I waited for a few seconds hoping he would elaborate his answer with more than just a yes. When I saw that he didn't, I decided to continue on.

"Well I thought we were going to lunch this afternoon. You had me make the reservation a week ago." I sat up in bed and stared him down as he hastily got dressed.

"Fucking cancel it Samantha, I have somewhere I gotta be." I closed my eyes and shook my head. Jumping out of bed, I decided I wasn't even in the mood for an argument with him.

I busied myself making the bed as I ignored him. I wished silently that I could rid myself of this poor excuse of a marriage and my poor excuse of a husband.

"What, you mad?" he asked me as he buttoned his shirt, looking over in my direction.

Choosing not to say anything, I began making my way to the bathroom so that I could see about my hygiene. But Adam stood in my way so that I couldn't get by him.

"You better stop with all that attitude Samantha," he said as he pointed his index finger in my face, damn near poking my eye out.

Silence was all that he got when I stood and folded my arms waiting for him to get the fuck out of my way.

"You know this ghetto attitude you picked up is getting real fucking old, you know that?" he said, as he suddenly grabbed my face in his hands.

I was expecting this response from him, so I toughened up, showing him that he wasn't about to break me. Not today, fuck that.

"I'll be back tonight, or tomorrow. Whichever one I feel like." He roughly released my face and headed out through the bedroom door.

I marched inside of the bathroom picking my cell phone up off the dresser as I did. As I brushed my teeth, I dialled Selah's number.

"Sister, what's up?" Selah said as she answered my call.

"What time are you and Lamar going to the party? Do you mind coming by to get me?"

THE WELCOME BACK party for King was in full swing, with only one problem... King was nowhere to be seen.

Kwana greeted me with a warm hug asking me twenty million questions when we arrived. She shoved Kaden in my arms and I swore he got even cuter than the last time I saw him.

"So are you gonna tell me how you know King's sister and why she was comfortable letting you hold her son?" Selah asked. We were standing in a corner of Kwana's living room. Lamar was off conversing with some of the guys, leaving Selah and I alone.

My eyes kept scanning the room looking for King. Kwana said he got held up but he would be here shortly.

"It's a long story Selah. I'll tell you some other time," I answered her question without really answering it. She gave me a glare letting me know she knew something was up.

"By the way, you look as though you took extra care in getting dressed. You tryna impress somebody?" I scoffed at her and looked down at what I was wearing.

I tried to keep it simple by trying not to look too extra. I wore a blue and black, plaid shirt dress with a pair of knee-high, black boots on my feet. My short bob hairstyle was worn straight and I wore little make-up. I sprayed the same fragrance I wore two years ago when last King and I were together…Juicy Couture.

"Don't be silly, who would I be getting dressed up for." I brushed her off as I took a sip of my Cîroc.

"That's what I'm asking you bitch. You've been acting sneaky all damn day." I looked over at her and rolled my eyes dramatically, hoping she would drop it.

I was about to respond to her when I began hearing what sounded like cheering. Selah and I looked over in the direction of where all the mayhem was, and there he stood.

King walked into the packed living room looking like a walking, talking, handsome sin. A sin I wanted to commit over and over again!

He wore all white; a pair of white distressed jeans that hung low a little, a white Polo button-up T-shirt, and a pair of white, old school Nikes. His newly formed muscles bulged as his T-shirt clung to his body, and his beard looked as if he had just left the barber.

My body reacted to his presence immediately and I licked my

lips lustfully. My happiness turned to dismay when I saw he had a female with him, looked like the same chick I saw him with at the mall.

"Let me say this Sammie, if I wasn't involved with Lamar, I would suck the skin off Kingsale's dick," Selah whispered in my ear and I looked over at her in shock.

"Sammie, I heard he got a big ole Jamaican cocky," she said that shit in the worst Caribbean accent ever and I couldn't help but laugh.

"You stupid Selah, I swear," I told her as I turned my attention back to King. He was greeting his guests and his sister walked up to him and gave him a hug.

The way the bitch he was with was gripping a hold of his hand, one would have sworn someone was trying to steal him from her. She was pissing me off and I didn't even know why. I had no claims to King, so I shouldn't even be jealous right about now. But I was any damn way!

I couldn't take my eyes off him as he made his way through the guests. And just as if he could feel my eyes on him, he turned and looked right at me.

I didn't know how to feel or what to think as we stared at each other. Kwana looked over at where he was looking and smiled at me before speaking in his ear. I had no idea what she told him but he was walking over in our direction. Not before telling his little female friend to stay put.

"Oh damn, Sammie, is he coming over here?" Selah asked as she squeezed my hand. I fought to remain calm and not act as if I wanted to freak out, but inside I was screaming.

"Hey Selah, I'm glad you could make it. I see you brought along your sister. Hello Mrs. Daniel," King said as he nodded his head at me.

The whole Mrs. Daniel thing was getting old to me. I mean, that really was my name, but King was just being an ass by calling me that.

"Hello Kingsale." Two could play at this game; he preferred me to call him King. He cut his eyes at me before turning back to Selah.

"Where yo' nigga at? I need to holla at him about something," he said to Selah, who began looking around the room to locate Lamar.

She eventually saw him chatting with a hoochie mama and pointed him out to King.

"I know Lamar got me fucked up. Who the fuck is that big, fake booty bitch he's talking to?" Selah fussed as she kept eye-balling Lamar and the chick he was speaking with.

The last thing I needed was for Selah to wild out; she would shut this party down with her funky ass attitude.

"Girl, I'm sure it's nothing. He knows you're crazy so he won't do anything right under your nose, chill out," I said to her as I reached in to give her a re-assuring hug. She seemed to relax for a bit and she calmed down a little.

The rest of the day went by almost as if in slow motion. King was busy entertaining his people so much that I hardly saw him. We made eye contact a couple times throughout the day, but that was it.

I never attempted to reach out to him. I stayed away, giving him his space and respecting the fact that he was with someone.

The tension between Lamar and Selah was evident. Every chance Selah got she was in Lamar's ear about the chick he was talking to earlier. I was beginning to have enough of this day and thought maybe I was wrong for coming.

"I need to run and use the bathroom for a quick minute Selah," I said in her ear as I held on to her elbow.

She just nodded her head in response and I turned and walked away, relieved to give her and Lamar some space.

I attended to my business in the bathroom and stood washing my hands when I heard the door open.

Thinking that I may have forgotten to lock the door, I looked up at the mirror and froze at the reflection behind me.

King stood at the door closing it and locking it behind him.

Our eyes locked in the mirror above the sink, and I remained stuck to the spot, the water running over my hands.

"Um, I was about to be done," I said as I regained my composure and turned off the faucet.

King's eyes swooped over my body and he bit into his lower lip as he walked to where I stood.

Standing directly behind me, I saw his eyes were bloodshot red and he smelled like weed and alcohol.

We stood in silence as I felt his body heat emanating from his body to mine. I shut my eyes as his hand roughly slapped my ass, the sound bouncing off the walls of the small space we stood in.

"You letting another nigga hit this? Why this shit spread out like butter?" he asked me as his hand massaged my butt cheeks. I opened my eyes so that I could look at his face in the mirror.

He concentrated hard on my ass as his hands continued their assault of rubbing me vigorously.

"I haven't been with anybody, King, and stop that." I reached and took hold of his hand pushing it away from my body.

"What, you don't like it when I touch you? Who else you letting touch you?" He glared at me angrily from the mirror before he held me by my upper arm and turned me to face him.

"Why you care who touches me, you rolled up in here with a chick on your arm, right?" I asked him, cursing myself for sounding like a jealous girlfriend.

He smiled at me. Reaching up, he held me from behind my neck, his eyes focused on my lips that were now slightly open.

"I missed the fuck out of you, you know that Sammie." The way he said my name, the way he massaged my neck and the way his eyes were glued on my lips, was doing something to my insides.

"I'm sorry I never visited you. I wanted to so many times. I felt awful that you got locked up that night. I felt as though somehow it was my fault." He placed his index finger to my lips to silence me.

"Don't say that baby. I wasn't expecting you to come visit me. That would have been too risky, and don't you ever think what happened that night was your fault. You hear me?" He began lowering his head to mine, our lips inches apart.

"I missed you too, King." I admitted to him just as his lips reached mine. We kissed each other with a fever like no other. Our tongues colliding and entwining as though we couldn't get enough of each other.

"I don't even give a fuck who's outside, I want to be inside you." he said. Not waiting for a response from me, he grabbed the hem of my dress and pulled it up above my waist.

His hand found my dripping pussy and rubbed on me from between my panties. I groaned loudly into his mouth as his fingers dipped inside of my underwear parting my pussy lips, so he could circle my throbbing clit.

"I missed your scent," he said as he sniffed behind my ear where I sprayed my perfume. "I missed your taste." He removed his fingers from between my thighs and placed them in his mouth as he sucked on them.

"Turn around." He placed his hands on my shoulders and spun me back around to face the mirror.

Getting on his knees, he hoisted my dress over my ass and slowly pulled down my underwear. I stepped out of them and he ran his hands down the back of my thighs.

With my eyes shut I enjoyed the illicit encounter King and I were about to partake in. I felt his lips place butterfly kisses from the back of my knees, straight to my ass. I cried out when I felt his teeth sink into my flesh.

Parting my butt cheeks, he ran his tongue between my cheeks, circling my anus. I grabbed a hold of the sink, curling my lips in an effort not scream out as if I was being murdered.

"Lift your leg up Sammie," he said in a commanding tone, and I wasted no time to do as I was told.

Hoisting my leg up to the edge of the sink, I bit into my arm as King proceeded to eat my pussy out from the back. His tongue dipped in and out from my slit, then wrapped itself around my clit and sucked on it as it pulsed in his mouth.

"Mmmmmmm," I groaned as he began fucking me with his tongue. "King, you about to make me cum...shit!" I cried out as I felt my orgasm building. Before I could get mine he moved away standing up behind me.

"Na, I want you to cum with my dick buried deep inside you," he said as he freed his dick from his jeans. Placing his rock-hard erection at my entrance, it felt like he was about to give me raw dick. I began to panic and tried to push him away.

"King, don't you have any condoms?" I said as I looked back at him.

"Na, I don't, but I'm tryna fuck Sammie, with or without a rubber." Using the tip of his dick he began rubbing it back and forth at my opening and my stupid ass forgot all about safe sex.

I rocked my ass back, inviting him to fuck me, rubber or not. Pressing his dick against my pussy, he eased himself in hissing and mumbling curse words as he did so.

I bit into my bottom lip as he stretched my walls, revelling in how fucking wonderful he felt.

"Sammie, this fucking pussy right here..." Not completing his sentence, he pushed his length in, sucking in his breath as he did so.

Using his hands, he steadied me by holding on to my waist and plunged inside of me.

"King," I gasped, realizing just how much I missed him. As he fucked me hard, my ass slapped loudly against his thigh.

"Don't nobody else allowed to get this pussy, you heard me. You heard me Sammie?" he asked me as he slapped my ass painfully.

"Yes, King," I replied breathlessly.

"I fucking mean it Sammie." He pounded me even harder and I bit into my bottom lip, drawing blood. He reached up and pulled my hair, forcing my head to tilt all the way back.

"Fucking nobody allowed to touch you, not even your husband." I moaned in ecstasy as I felt his middle finger begin circling my anus, before pressing gently inside of it.

I was losing my fucking mind as King never slowed down, his strokes slamming my body forward over and over violently.

Reaching between us he rubbed on my clit, using my wetness as lubrication as he circled my bud. Gripping the sides of the sink tightly I gasped loudly as my orgasm rocked my entire body.

"Shit, I can't hold this nut any longer. Fuck Sammie, I missed you baby." He groaned as his body shook and I felt his warmth filling up my insides.

"You got the sweetest *punanny* Sammie," he said against my ear as he pulled out of me, stopping to place a kiss on my back.

King and I cleaned up our secretions in silence, smiling with each other whenever our eyes made contact.

"I'm so sorry to hear about your mother. May she rest in peace." I reached up and caressed his upper arm. He looked at me and smiled softly.

"Appreciate it," he said.

Looking for my clutch, I picked it up from off the floor and opened it. I took out something that I believed King would be wanting and held my hand out to give it to him.

Looking at what I was offering, King began shaking his head at me, which left me a bit baffled.

"It's yours. I'm giving it back to you," I said to him as I held my hand out with his chain.

"Na, the time ain't right to give that back to me just yet." I creased my forehead as he shoved his hands inside of his pockets refusing to take his chain back.

"I don't understand."

"When the time is really right to return that to me, you'll know." Lifting my chin up, he bent his head and kissed my lips. "I'm about to go on back outside." Turning, he made his way to the door and grabbed hold of the knob. Before he opened it, he turned to me again.

"I meant what I said. I missed you Sammie." My heart fluttered in my chest as King turned and walked out the door. I was all in my fucking feelings as I put his chain away and checked my refection in the mirror, making sure I didn't look a hot mess.

I walked back out into the festivities finding Selah in the exact spot I left her.

"Where the fuck have you been Sammie?" she asked me, sounding even more irritated than when I left her.

"I told you, I had to use the bathroom," I said to her, trying my best to avoid eye contact with her so she wouldn't suspect anything was up.

That did not fucking work. She began eyeing me up and down,

narrowing her eyes at me in suspicion. This dummy even sniffed me a little.

"Sammie!" she said loudly, gasping at me. "Did you have sex?" she asked me as my eyes grew wide as I stared back at her.

"What! Are you insane Selah?" I said to her as I laughed nervously.

"You a whole liar. Who the fuck was it?" I huffed out an annoyed breath as I looked away from her prying eyes. "It's King isn't it?" she asked me, and I looked back at her wondering if she had some sort of sixth sense.

"No," I lied, knowing damn well I wasn't a good liar.

"Bitch, I done put two and two together. His sister knows you and you found the bathroom real good on your own just now without any directions. You better spill the tea." I groaned loudly and looked around for Lamar.

"Where's Lamar?" I asked her, not about to reveal anything for the fear of being heard.

"I cussed him out and he went outside or wherever." She waved her hand around as if she was unbothered.

I exhaled loudly, knowing I would have to confide in her because she wouldn't let it go until I did.

"What I'm about to tell you, don't repeat this shit to anybody," I said through clenched teeth as I spoke in her ear.

I knew I could trust my sister, so I began to confide in her about what really was going down between King and me.

Selah

"**Y**ou got me fucked Lamar," I said, as I mushed the side of his head as he drove us home.

"You better stop with all the fucking dramatics, Selah," he said, as he turned briefly to scowl at me before turning his eyes back on the road.

"I can't stand your disrespectful ass. You were all up in that bitch's face as if you didn't go up in there with me. Why you always gotta embarrass me Lamar?" I asked, as if I was actually about to get an honest response.

"I told you I know the bitch from around, I just went to say hey. I don't see why you trippin'." I swear I wanted nothing more than to mush his big head again but I was afraid we might fuck around and crash.

I remained silent for the remainder of the ride, cursing the day I met Lamar.

At the time we met I worked at a doctor's office as a receptionist. Lamar walked in looking like a tall glass of caramel Frappuccino because I loved my men a little lighter in complexion. It's just my preference.

I'm not about to lie but he wasn't the one that came in to see the doctor; it was actually his girlfriend at the time that had the appointment.

While she was inside talking to the doctor, Lamar stayed out in the waiting room. He sat directly opposite my reception desk and I was stealing glances his way every second I got.

He was tall, his long legs stretched casually out in front of him. His hair was braided in four corn-rows going all back. His neck had a tattoo of a hundred-dollar bill to the front. He had these pair of big ole Jay-Z type lips but his were sexy and fit him perfectly.

He wore a long-sleeved shirt that day but I just knew his body was probably filled with tattoos which were my weakness. I just loved a bad boy that was tatted up. And I could tell that Lamar was the bad boy type; he gave out that aura.

The work phone rang and I answered with the usual greeting. As I was making an appointment for one of our usual patients I looked up and Lamar was staring at me.

We held each other's gaze as I spoke on the phone; he licked his lips a couple times and smiled at me slightly. I remember blushing like crazy, feeling my insides grow warm.

His girlfriend returned and he got up and walked over to her. She seemed upset and I heard her say she was about to go wait for him in the car. She stormed out of the office without even giving him a second look.

He came to my desk to pay for her visit and took out this big wad of cash.

"What's your name?" he asked, as I wrote up his receipt.

"Selah," I replied, feeling my face flush with excitement.

"Why don't you go ahead and write your number on the back of my receipt for me," he said, sounded as cool as ever.

Of course, I should have known right then and there that a nigga that would ask for another female's number with his girlfriend right outside, was a nigga you should definitely leave alone.

Obviously, I went ahead and gave his stupid ass my number anyway. Turned out his girlfriend found out she was pregnant at her doctor's visit, Lamar said she accused of him of knocking her up on purpose, and she had an abortion behind his back. So he called off the relationship because he said he wanted her to have the baby.

We started messing around after he broke it off with her and we'd been together since. That was about eight months ago and shit had been a fucking nightmare for a couple months now.

Lamar encouraged me to quit my job, saying he made more than enough money selling dope and hustling, so he would prefer I not work.

That whole he'd take care of me bullshit didn't last very long. He started giving me little to no money, started staying out really late, and sometimes he didn't even bother to come home.

When I questioned him about where he spent the night at he would say he slept over at his own apartment since he lived over at my house. This always happened; I kept letting these fuck-boy types into my life. I just wished I could meet someone to give me the type of love I wanted.

I exhaled loudly as we pulled up to my three-bedroom home. My parents helped me buy this house and I adored the fuck out of it.

Lamar parked his car in the driveway and I wasted no time in hopping out, slamming his door in the process.

I opened the door with my keys and walked down the corridor to my bedroom. I stripped out of my clothes and made my way to my bathroom.

As I stood under the shower enjoying the way the warm water felt against my skin, I heard Lamar enter the bathroom. I looked through the glass door and he was naked about to climb in with me. I waited until I felt him to the back of me rubbing his hands on my ass, and I sucked my teeth and walked out of the shower leaving his ass standing there alone.

I towel dried myself and was applying lotion to my skin when he walked inside of the bedroom.

"You wanna play hard to get?" he asked, as he walked closer to where I stood rubbing lotion to my naked body.

"Who says I am playing?" I raised my eyebrows at him giving him attitude.

Now standing to the front of me, he took the bottle of lotion from out my hand. Squeezing some into his palm as he began rubbing it into my breasts slowly, his index and thumb stopping to lightly tweak at my nipples.

His hand slowly travelled down my stomach, rubbing in a circular motion.

"Why you always getting mad at a nigga? You know I care about you right?" he asked, as his hand moved down even more to my pulsing pussy.

I looked at him as he used one hand to part my pussy lips while he used his middle finger on his other hand to make slow circles on my clit.

Dipping his finger inside my wetness, he used it to coat my clit, his finger gliding around it even faster.

"Lamar," I moaned just as his lips found mine.

Lamar was an expert with both his tongue and his fingers. He continued kissing me deeply while his fingers brought me to an orgasm that made my knees all wobbly.

Wrapping his hand around my neck, he removed his lips from mine. "Now get your ass on that bed so I can show you how much I care about your hostile ass."

<hr />

"I DON'T EVEN KNOW why you decided to get another job," Lamar fussed as he dropped me off at my new receptionist job.

I rolled my eyes at his stupid statement as he parked in the parking lot of the gynecologist office where I'd be working.

"I miss working and we could use the extra money Lamar," I said, as I grabbed up my Gucci purse and looked at myself in the mirror making sure my face looked right.

"The block has been a little slow baby, but things will pick up." I rolled my eyes and opened the door and climbed out.

"Bye, don't forget to pick me up at five," I told him as I was about to close the door.

"Don't you think your skirt is a little short, Selah?" I looked down at my red skirt that stopped just above my knees. I wore it with a white ruffled shirt that was tucked neatly in my skirt with a pair of red pumps. My box braids hung just above my ass and I flipped my hair over my shoulder.

"Boy, quit playing. Besides, the gynecologist is a female. See you later," I said as I walked toward the building.

As I entered through the door I was expecting to see the Ob/Gyn Sharon Smith who interviewed me for my position. Instead, sitting at the reception desk was a man. For a split second I swore I walked through the wrong door and I paused my steps.

"Um, good morning. I was hoping to find Mrs. Sharon Smith, I'm her new receptionist," I said as I smiled sweetly.

"You're late," the stranger that I did not know responded.

Trying not to bring out my inner gangster, I took a deep breath and looked at the watch on my wrist. I had to report to work at eight and it was only 7:50.

"No, I'm not late and I'm sorry, who are you?" I asked as I looked him up and down.

I took a step back as he stood up and walked toward me, and I used this opportunity to have a good look at him. He was tall and had a complexion that reminded me of a cup of Ovaltine. He had a pair of brown eyes that were nice and bright. His hair was cut low and had a lot of waves, he had no facial hair, and his lips were full and pink.

His work shirt hugged his muscular biceps and firm chest, and the pair of black work pants he wore clung to his toned legs, letting me know he was no stranger to the gym.

God sure as hell took his sweet time when he created this man, I thought as he held his hand out to me.

"I'm Ob/Gyn Jaime Francis, and maybe Mrs. Smith should have explained that this is a shared office." I blinked my eyes repeatedly at him as we shook each other's hand. Shared office, what the hell?

"I don't understand. How do you even share an office, is she your wife?" I asked, feeling totally lost.

"No she isn't, she's my sister. She works Mondays and Thursdays and I work Tuesday, Wednesday and Fridays." I brought my eyebrows together.

"But today is Monday, so why isn't she here?" I asked as Jaime's eyes swept over my attire making me think Lamar could have been right about the length of my skirt.

"She needed to leave the country for a couple of months suddenly. So I'll be here every day until she returns. With that being said, you are to report to work no later than 7:30am. Please inform me when my first patient arrives." Saying nothing more, he spun around and walked inside of his office closing the door behind him.

I stood speechless for a couple seconds before I made my way to my desk.

That was Mrs. Smith's brother, talk about polar opposites; they were nothing alike. For starters, Mrs. Smith looked nothing like him. She was short and light-skinned and very skinny. And she was way friendlier than Jaime, who seemed like a total asshole.

I sighed loudly as I powered on my computer. This was going to be a hell of a two months!

King

I was as nervous as a runaway slave. I stood next to my uncle as he knocked on the front door of Samantha and her husband's home.

I looked down at my appearance and I felt like a motherfucking penguin with my black slacks and white shirt with a pair of black Steve Madden shoes.

I didn't know what the fuck I was doing. Samantha still had no fucking clue I was about to replace my uncle and be their new driver.

"Why the fuck you look like you about to shit your liver out, King?" my uncle asked, and I turned to look at him, exhaling a nervous breath.

"Na, I'm cool," I said as I adjusted my shirt collar.

The door opened suddenly and there he stood, the nigga I hated and I didn't even know all that much about him. All I knew was that he was married to the woman I knew deep down that I had fallen in love with. And that was more than enough for me to hate his ass.

"Joseph, please come in," he said, but his eyes were on me and not my uncle. He allowed his eyes to slowly take all of me in as if I were some sort of pesky insect.

My uncle and I followed him through his living room to the back where he had his office. As we walked to his office, I spun my head around hoping that Samantha would appear…but she didn't.

"Please, have a seat. Kingsale, right?" he asked me as he closed the door and took a seat behind his desk.

Me and my uncle took a seat on the opposite side of him.

"Yes, Kingsale. It's nice to meet you Mr. Daniel," I lied, as I held my hand out for him to shake.

We shook hands very briefly and then he cleared his throat loudly.

"Well, Kingsale, your uncle has expressed to me that he would like you to take on his duties as being my driver," Adam said, with a tight, somewhat cold expression on his face. What exactly Samantha saw in him was confusing as fuck to me.

"Yes, that's correct." I had already begun getting bored with this whole conversation and wondered where Samantha was. I was hoping she would have been present in this meeting.

"Your uncle told me that you got into trouble with the law a little over two years ago. I am in no position to judge but I do hope you've put those thug ways behind you." I wanted to reach over this fucking table and punch a couple of his teeth down his throat.

I mean, who the fuck does this stuck-up nigga think he is, talking about thug ways. I ought to knock his head off his motherfucking shoulders.

"Yes, Mr. Daniel, my thug days are long behind me," I replied, as I held his gaze.

"Good, the last thing I need is for you to make the news dragging me along with you." The more I listened to this donkey, the more I kept thinking I would enjoy taking Samantha away from him.

"Well since your uncle recommended you, I am more than willing to give you the opportunity. You are not required to work every day, just the days when I need to attend important meetings or conferences. My wife has her own means of transportation but there will be days when she may need you." I chuckled to myself at the last part he said. He just had no idea how much she needed me.

"OK, I understand. Do I get to meet your wife today?" I asked, hoping that I didn't sound too enthusiastic.

"Yes, let me go get her. I told her she needed to be down here because I had something I needed to discuss with her. But you know how women can be stubborn." I clenched my jaw, the only thing that would help me to remain silent.

I watched as Mr. Daniel excused himself and made his way to the office door and disappeared through it.

"King, remember to be on your best behavior. Mr. Daniel was kind enough to give you a second chance, so don't fuck this up." I looked over at my uncle, wanting nothing more than to hit him upside his head; acting like an Uncle Tom.

"Yeah, aight unc," I said with a shrug of my shoulder, not enjoying the way he spoke to me as if I was some sort of toddler.

Mr. Daniel suddenly walked into the room and I looked behind him as Samantha followed him. She didn't notice me at first because she was paying attention to my uncle.

I stood up so that I could formally greet her and that's when her eyes settled on me. I could see the shocked expression she tried to hide as my uncle stood next to me, and her husband stood at her side.

"Kingsale Rock, I'd like to officially introduce you to my wife, Samantha Daniel." With a forced smile on her lips Samantha held her hand out to me.

"It's a pleasure meeting you again, Kingsale," she said, as I shook her hand. I smiled as I admired how beautiful she looked. She wore an all-black pants suit with a red shirt under her jacket and a pair of red pumps on her feet. Red heels were the sexiest thing a woman could wear in my opinion.

"It's nice meeting you again, Mrs. Daniel," I said, as I looked her in her eyes.

"Oh yeah, I forgot you two would have met before," Mr. Daniel said as he placed his hand on the middle of her back. I suddenly got the urge to tell him keep his hand to his fucking self, but I wasn't trying to get fired before I even started working.

"Well now that we're all caught up, Samantha, are you still going downtown this morning?" I looked over at her, as both myself and her husband waited on her response.

"Ye-yes, I am." I smiled at the way she stuttered; it meant that I was making her nervous, and I liked that.

"Well good, let Kingsale take you. I have some business to talk about with Joseph." Samantha suddenly got a panicked look on her face as she looked over at her husband.

"Don't you have to go to your office? You'll need him more. I can take my own car," she replied as she shook her head. Damn, if shorty didn't calm her ass down her husband may become suspicious.

"No, don't worry about it. I may work late tonight anyway so I'll need my own ride." There was a flash of disappointment on her face at hearing him say he would be working late. Which reminded me of the first time we met when she cried in the back of the limo.

"I don't mind taking you Mrs. Daniel," I said as I gave her an intense look, and I could tell that she felt uncomfortable.

"Ok," was all she said as her lips formed a tight line. "Let me just run upstairs and grab my purse." Samantha turned and bolted out the office so fast, I swore her ass suddenly caught on fire.

"Here, it's the black Bentley parked out front," Mr. Daniel said as he handed me a car key. I gave him a head nod as I shook my uncle's hand, and he gave me a hard warning glare. Turning, I walked out the room back out the way we came in.

I walked out the front door toward the black Bentley parked to the front of the house. I unlocked the door and sat down inside admiring the interior. I knew Mr. Daniel was a councilman and all, but he was living as though he was Denzel Washington or somebody.

I looked up at the house and thought to myself, it was pretty large for a councilman's home. Had me wondering if Mr. Daniel was doing some extra hustling on the side.

I smiled to myself as the front door opened suddenly and Samantha stepped out, looking fine as fuck as her newly swollen hips swung from left to right in her pants suit that hugged her curvy body as she approached the car.

I could tell she was about to jump up my ass by the expression on her face.

She slammed the door as she sat in the back seat.

"Just drive, King," she said. Her face held a stone-cold expression as I looked back at her in the rear-view mirror.

Starting the car, I pulled out of the long driveway and into the street.

"What the hell is wrong with you? Is this some type of game to you or something?" *And so it begins*, I thought, smiling to myself.

"Good morning to you too, Samantha...oh, I mean Sammie," I said, as I continued glancing at her every couple seconds but making sure I kept my eyes on the road. The last thing I needed was to fuck around and crash the first day on the job.

"King, what the hell is this?" she asked sounding panicked, as if she was about to have some sort of anxiety attack.

"What you mean baby?" I used the word baby just to fuck with her, and it worked. Her eyeballs got as big as grapefruits as she gawked at me in shock.

"I am completely convinced you've gone mad," she said with a vigorous shake of her head.

I chuckled at her silliness and asked for directions on where she was headed.

"Just take the fastest route to downtown and I'll direct from you there," she told me, finally sounding a bit more relaxed.

We remained silent for the next few minutes as I became lost in my thoughts. Samantha cleared her throat loudly before she began speaking.

"How come you grew a beard? I've been meaning to ask you," she said, making me smile at her question.

"I wanted to look older." I smirked as I saw her roll her eyes, but she smiled anyway.

"Did I tell you how much I loved how your hips are filling out everything you wear?" She looked at me in the rear-view mirror as our eyes locked.

"You don't think I look fat?" she asked, as she looked down at her perfect body.

"You could never look too fat to me, Sammie," I replied to her in all honesty. This woman could never look bad in my books. I loved everything about her.

"Adam seems to think I've gained too much weight." I clenched my jaw tightly as soon as those words passed her lips.

"Yeah, well Adam's an asshole, so fuck that *batty boy*," I said; my Jamaican accent sounded thick as I used the slang.

"What does *batty boy* mean anyway?" Samantha asked, as she giggled after saying the word.

"It means he's a gay fuck-boy." Samantha gasped at the meaning but started giggling again. That sound was the best sound I'd heard all damn day.

"You're crazy, you do know that right?" She shook her head at me.

"I'm crazy about you." She got extremely quiet at what I said and I silently cursed myself because I didn't want her to think I was some sort of weirdo.

"You don't mean that," Samantha said as she turned and looked out her window.

"How you about to tell me what I mean and don't mean. There wasn't a day that went by over the last two years that I didn't think about you. And it's not because you have the best *punanny* a nigga ever had. It's just something about you. I just want to always be around you or something." I suddenly felt like a pussy expressing the way I felt about Samantha who was very much married, not to mention three years my senior.

"King, you don't know what you're saying. I think you're confusing lust with whatever it is that you think you feel for me." I exhaled loudly, frustrated that Samantha kept brushing off how I felt about her as if I was a child that didn't understand his feelings.

"You fucking bugging, Sammie. Where are we going anyway?" I asked her, deciding I was done expressing to her how I felt. I wasn't about to let her disregard my feelings and make me feel like a punk.

"Make a left at the corner," she said as she pointed to the street I was approaching. I followed her directions having no clue as to where we were going.

"It's right after that little restaurant." I stopped the car and looked at the building that sat next to the restaurant. I creased my eyebrows when I saw the *for rent* sign that hung from the window.

I looked back at Samantha, confused as to why she needed to be here.

"What's this about?" I asked as she pulled on the door handle and pushed it open. At the same time, a woman emerged from the front door of the building and Samantha walked up to her and shook her hand.

Turning off the engine, I hopped out the car as if somebody invited my ass to come along.

"Mrs. Daniel, so nice to see you again," the woman said as she shook Samantha's hand. I stood next to them as the lady turned and eyed me suspiciously.

"Um, is this Mr. Daniel?" I scrunched my nose up at her. The audacity of her to mistake me for that dickhead of a husband Samantha had.

"Hell no, I'm King," I said as I corrected her, hearing Samantha gasp as if she wasn't yet used to me saying what came to my mind.

"Oh, well, hello King, it's a pleasure to meet you, I'm Mrs. Susan Bell. Can we go in?" she asked as she extended her hand out, showing Samantha the way through the front door.

Samantha smiled and walked through the door and Mrs. Bell walked in after her. As I said before, nobody invited my ass to be a part of whatever this was, but that didn't stop a nigga from tagging along.

As I stepped inside of the room, I came to see that it was just a big, empty space. I looked over at Samantha who had the biggest smile on her lips as her eyes eagerly took in the spacious room.

"So, Mrs. Daniel, this is quite an adequate amount of space don't you think?" Mrs. Bell asked she walked across the empty room.

"Yes, it's just what I need," Samantha replied just as Mrs. Bell's cell phone rang. She excused herself, saying that it was an important call, and stepped out from the room.

"What's this about Sammie?" I asked as I wandered around the room, curious as to what she wanted with this empty spot.

"I would like to buy it. I wanna open my very own yoga studio."

Samantha

*W*as that all it took for King to be speechless, was for me to mention opening my own yoga studio? Because he was standing, staring at me with his mouth wide open.

"Aye," I said as I snapped my fingers in front of his face. "Why look so shocked, don't you think I have it in me to open my very own business?" I asked as I placed my hand on my hip, kind of pissed that he seemed so shocked at what I said.

"I would never think you don't have it in you to be independent. I'm just pleasantly surprised is all. I never even knew you did yoga." King took a step closer to me and I bit into the insides of my cheek.

From the moment I saw him back at my home, my stomach had been in knots. Even though I was beyond mad that he went about working for us in a sneaky manner, I was low-key happy that I would be seeing more of him even though it would be risky.

"I took up yoga after you got arrested," I said as I confided in him. "I stopped a few months ago which is how I gained these extra pounds." I looked down at my body and smiled at my rounded hips.

"Teach this Jamaican boy a little yoga nah," King said, his accent sounding heavier than usual. I couldn't help but laugh at the way he said that.

"Are you sure you're flexible enough?" I questioned him with a suggestive raise of my eyebrow. I took a step back and unbuttoned the jacket I wore so that I could get more comfortable. I took my heels off and pushed them to the side. Folding my jacket, I laid it on top of my shoes.

"Ah shit, let me get ready," King said as he began to rotate neck while he stretched his hand outward as he cracked his interlocked fingers.

"You are so silly." I laughed as I positioned myself on the floor. "Ok, so this position is called The Child Pose." I crouched my knees in under me, resting my forehead on the floor with my arms outstretched in front of me.

To the right of me, I saw King got in the same position as he struggled to keep the pose.

"Fuck, this shit hurts like a motherfucker," he mumbled, and I tilted my head to the side so that I could get a better look at him.

"This position helps with neck and back pain, and it also helps calm and relax you." I took a deep breath and exhaled slowly as King and I looked at each other. A warm sensation rushed through my body as King's eyes filled with lust.

Deciding I was going to turn things up a notch and have some fun with him, I stood up.

I waited for him to do the same as he got up to his feet. We stood facing each other and a mischievous smile spread across my face.

"This position is called The Bridge." I raised my hands above my head and King did the same, but I shook my head at him. "I think you may have to sit this one out big boy." Flicking my wrist back so that the palms of my hands faced the ceiling, I flipped my body backward so that the palms of my hands were now flat on the floor.

My body formed what looked like backward C, my hips were thrust in the air in a forward motion.

"*Boomboclat*, Sammie," King said as I took deep breaths.

"This position helps to strengthen your spine, relieves stress, anxiety and insomnia. It also improves spinal flexibility." From my upside-down view I saw King come to stand in front of my pretzel type body.

"I really like this view, Sammie." I smiled to myself seeing that my attempt to get his attention was a success.

Taking my time, I inched my hands out so that I could regain my standing posture. I stood up and exhaled loudly, King and I now standing very close to each other.

"Want me to show you one more?" I asked as he bit lustfully into his lower lip.

"Yes, please," he said, his pupils dilating to a darker shade of brown. I turned my back to him, raised my hands above my head again and dropped my palms flat on the floor in front of me.

With my palms on the ground and my butt high in the air, I looked between my thighs at King's legs.

"This is called, The Downward Dog." My ass was directly in line with King's crotch and he placed his hand on my hip and I felt his dick against my booty.

Enjoying this way more than I should, I scooted back a bit so that my ass was now right up on his crotch.

"Sammie, don't play with a nigga like this." I heard the longing in his voice as he massaged his hand into my ass.

Pushing myself upward, I stood up keeping my back to his front and he wrapped his arms securely around my waist. I placed my hand on top of his and pushed my body even further against him.

With his lips pressed on my ear, King said words that made my heart skip a beat. "I want you all to myself."

I closed my eyes and allowed King to turn me around to face him. Not even bothering to open my eyes, I moaned as I felt King's lips crush on to my own. I instinctively wrapped my arms around his neck and opened my mouth allowing his tongue to clash with mine.

"I want you to myself, Sammie," he whispered against my lips. His hand inching in between my thighs, moving slowly to my pulsing pussy.

"Mmmm, King," I groaned inside his mouth as his fingers gently squeezed my kitty.

"Ahem!" The sound of someone clearing their throat interrupted our kiss, prompting the both of us to pull away from each other.

I turned to Mrs. Bell looking at King and I with a slightly embarrassed expression on her face. Mrs. Bell knew I was very much a married woman and she knew King wasn't my husband.

I pulled away from King, ashamed of the way he made me act like some sort of lovesick puppy.

"I'll be in the car," King said as he turned and walked out the door without another word.

I walked to where my jacket and shoes were, putting them on quickly.

"I was just showing King some yoga moves," I told Mrs. Bell, not even sure why I felt like I needed to explain myself to her.

Raising her palms up, she said, "Hey, I'm not here to judge. I'm just here to show you this spot. Now, shall we continue?" Giving her a tight smile, I followed her into the next room.

Fifteen minutes later I walked out of the building thanking Mrs. Bell for showing me around.

"I'll let you know what I decide before the end of the month. Hopefully it will still be available," I told her as we shook hands before we parted ways.

I made my way to the car and opened the door and sat down at the back. Bob Marley was playing softly as King sang along with the lyrics.

He turned to look at me, his eyes roaming boldly over my body. "Where am I taking you now Empress?"

I loved that name he called me so much, my lips immediately formed a smile.

"Home I guess; this was all I really had to do today." I shrugged my shoulders. I didn't have my own profession like my husband. He told me being married to him, I didn't need a job of my own. Something I instantly regretted when he showed me his true colors.

"Home? Sammie, it's barely even mid-day. What the fuck do you plan on doing all day while that nigga's out the house?" I shrugged my shoulders absentmindedly, thinking I may sound pretty pathetic to King.

"I usually spend time with my sister, but she got a new job

recently. Or I take care of Adam's schedule for the rest of the week, let him know what meetings and agendas he has coming up." Even as the words passed my lips they sounded lame as hell, leading me to realize that I had no life and everything I did basically revolved around my cheating husband.

"I was about to go over to Kwana's, you down for that?" King asked, not even bothering to wait for my response. He started the car and drove off.

"So you about to open your own yoga studio? I think that's a very good idea. I'm impressed, Sammie." I smiled at him but King didn't know the half of it.

"I guess you can say it's all just wishful thinking," I replied in a melancholy tone as I turned to look out the window.

"What you mean by that?" he asked me.

"I don't have enough money saved to purchase the building and if I ask Adam, he's going to ask two questions. First, why am I saving money in a separate account that he doesn't know about. And two, why am I thinking about opening my own business when he strictly forbade me to have my own career." King sucked his teeth loudly at me, as if what I said was the most ridiculous thing he ever heard.

"Yo, you living for yourself or you living for that nigga? Do what makes you happy, Sammie. If getting your yoga on makes you happy and you want to open up your own studio then go for it, fuck that nigga," King said as he drove in the direction of his sister's place, even though I never officially told his ass to take me there. I guess it was just King being King.

"How much do you need?" His question confused me and I turned to look at the back of his head.

"What do you mean how much do I need?" I asked.

"Like how much more money do you need to buy the studio? Damn, did you fall asleep back there?" I rolled my eyes because he was so rude and blunt with his words.

"I need ten thousand more. It's twenty thousand in total and I got ten thousand saved up already." I smiled as he pulled up in front of his sister's apartment, feeling low-key happy that King obviously didn't mind bringing me around his twin.

"Cool, come on; let's go inside." King got out and as usual, he didn't even make an attempt to open my door. His uncle used to always make sure to open and close my doors. King on the other hand...

Opening my door, I got out and followed him, stopping to glance back at the Bentley worried if it would be safe. I mean, we weren't exactly in Beverly Hills.

"Aye, nobody ain't about to fuck with your ride," King said as he raised his hand to a couple of fellas that stood on the corner. They waved their hand back in return as some form of secret communication that they would look after the car.

Knowing that King had weight in the streets, we continued walking toward Kwana's apartment door. King turned the knob and the door wasn't even locked and he walked right inside.

Kwana was playing music that just had to be Jamaican because I had no clue what the person was saying. She stood in the middle of her living room dancing with her son standing in front of her as he tried to imitate her dance moves.

"Why the fuck you teaching my nephew how to twerk?" King said as he reached down and scooped Kaden up in his arms. Kaden wrapped his arms around his uncle's neck and began giggling.

"Shut up, King. I was just teaching him our Jamaican culture," Kwana said as she playfully shoved her twin brother's upper arm. I smiled, loving the way they interacted with each other. They always acted like they couldn't stand each other but you could tell just how much they loved one another.

"Come here baby." Kwana reached for her son taking him out of King's arms.

"Why you taking my little man? Y'all about to go somewhere?" I sat on the sofa and Kwana approached me with an apologetic look on her face.

"Girl, I'm sorry; I didn't even say hello. How you doing, is my big-headed brother treating you right?" Kwana placed Kaden on my lap as she sat next to me.

My heart melted as Kaden looked up at me with his big, bright, brown eyes. I lovingly caressed his chubby cheeks as he murmured something in baby language.

"He really does like you," Kwana said as she looked at me.

"Your brother had a good first day on the job. He still don't open my doors for me though, but I guess I can live with that." I looked over at King who had a confused expression on his face as I bent and kissed Kaden on his cheek.

Kwana picked him up from off my lap and stood up facing her brother. "Nigga, how you gon' be someone's driver and not open the door for them? I know Mama raised you better than that," Kwana fussed at him, making me regret that I ever mentioned it.

"Shut up, Kwana," King snapped at her.

"You shut up big head, with your un-mannerly ass. I'm about to run out to the park with Kaden for a bit. I'll be back in an hour. Don't mess my place up either," she said, pointing a finger at King.

King walked his sister and nephew out, kissing them both before they left out the door, locking it behind them.

I looked at him as he made his way over to where I sat, dropping his body weight loudly next to me on the sofa. I tried my best to relax and not show just how much his presence of being next to me was affecting me. I wiped my sweaty palms across the lap of my pants.

The music was still playing in the background and I began nodding my head to the song. I knew it was a Jamaican artist that was singing because I had understood nothing of what was being sung.

"Hey," King said as he lightly brushed his fingers against my knee. "Take your jacket off and kick your heels to the side and relax." King massaged just above my knee as he tucked his lower lip in his mouth, resting his head on the back of the sofa.

Giving him a nervous smile, I unbuttoned my jacket and tossed it over on the arm rest of the sofa. Next, I took my heels off enjoying how it felt for my feet being free from my shoes.

King left his arm on my leg and I glanced over at him and he was just sitting there staring at me.

"It's impolite to stare," I said to him, but all he did was give me a seductive type of smile.

"Dance with me." His request caught me off guard and I looked over at him quizzically.

"What?" I asked as I laughed a little.

King got up and stood in front of me, he unbuttoned his white shirt and took it off, now wearing only his white vest that he wore under his shirt.

"I don't know how to dance to this, King," I said as I shook my head at him. Refusing to take no for an answer, he reached for my hand and tugged on it, encouraging me to stand to my feet.

Turning me roughly so that my back was to his front, King planted his hands on my waist and pressed his body into mine.

My breath hitched in my throat as I felt his hips do a slow, rotating type of motion, grinding his hard dick into my ass.

Instinctively I began returning his gyrations with my waist turning in a circular motion to the beat of the song.

"What is he singing about?" I asked as King placed his lips to the back of my neck and sucked gently on my skin.

"You want me to sing it for you?" I closed my eyes and nodded my head as King's teeth nipped my neck.

"Me gal bend over let me give yuh from back," King began reciting the lyrics of the song in my ear as his lower body continued grinding into mine. *"Me have the key to your pad-lock. Love you over and over you say baby nah stop. You sweat till you're weak..."*

The way he said those words in my ear and the way his body moved so seductively against mine, I couldn't suppress the moan that escaped my lips.

King's hand began making its way to the front of my pants and rubbed on my pussy through the material. I opened my legs so that he could have enough room to assault between my thighs.

Using one hand to squeeze my breasts and the other to slowly un-zip my pants, King had me calling out his name in record time.

I could hardly catch my breath as King shoved his hand down the front of my panties and rubbed on my clit. My pants fell to a puddle at my feet and I stepped out of them.

"King," I moaned out his name as he sucked on my earlobe, his fingers picking up the pace. Dipping his finger in and out of me and placing it back to my clit, I reached up so that I could place my hand to the back of his neck.

I thrust my hips forward loving the way his fingers tortured my throbbing pussy.

"Go sit down and open your pretty legs as wide as they can go," King said with a firm slap on my ass. With overcooked spaghetti legs I took a couple steps to the sofa. Before sitting, I began to take my underwear off.

King held his hand up. "Na, don't take those off. Just sit down." Not breaking his eye contact, I sat on the edge of the sofa and opened my legs. Usually I would have been bashful but there was something about King that made me want to be a naughty freak just for him.

Giving me a sly smile, he walked to the kitchen and came back with a glass filled with ice. One of the ice cubes was already in his mouth as he sucked on the chip.

Kneeling in front of me sucking on the ice, he held my gaze as he wasted no time caressing my pussy.

I closed my eyes and dipped my head back, my mouth opened, but not a single sound came out. King's fingers were cool to the touch as he rubbed on me through my underwear.

Placing his mouth close to my pussy, he blew his cold breath against me and I gasped at the sensation.

His lips began kissing my inner thigh, occasionally allowing the ice to replace his lips, as he made his way to my anticipating pussy.

"Aahhhh," I cried out as King shifted my panties out of his way so that he could wrap his cold tongue around my clit. I never knew the feel of something so cold against something so warm and sensitive could make me feel this good... I fucking loved it!

King held my legs opened with his hands on my knees as his entire mouth covered my pussy. He worked his mouth on me as if he was tongue kissing me down there.

He slurped noisily against my mound, driving me fucking insane as he moaned while he ate me out.

"Oh...my...god," I moaned softly, as I looked down at him as his tongue flicked against my bud. His eyes were closed as if he were in deep concentration about his duties.

Feeling my orgasm building, I placed my hand to the back of his head forcing his face further against me.

"Mmhmm...mmhmmm," he hummed as my body shook with my orgasm, forcing me to shut my eyes tightly.

"Shit, shit, shit," I cursed repeatedly as I breathlessly released inside of his mouth. King lapped slowly on my slit giving me time to climb down from cloud nine.

"Now, you can take this off," he said as he pulled my panties off me. I sat naked at the waist as King stood up and unzipped his pants, freeing his rod of correction.

I licked my lips as he told me to lay back on the sofa. Nestling his body between my legs, he took one of my legs and hiked it up on his shoulder.

I felt him place his tip at my opening, pushing past my tight skin. I put my hand on his chest. "You don't have protection?" I asked as I looked up at him. I swear my lips said those words but my body inched up wanting to feel all of him in me.

"I'mma pull out. I really need to be inside you right now, Sammie." With those final words he rammed himself inside of me causing me to bite into my bottom lip.

"Fuck, baby. I love this fucking *pum pum*, you know that?" King pumped in and out of me as he looked down between our bodies, obviously enjoying the view of him pumping in and out of me, stretching me out.

Holding my elevated leg at the back of my thigh, he pushed my leg even further back. Thank god for my yoga skills!

"You make my dick so fucking hard, Sammie. I can't get enough of your ass." I clawed at his back as I listened to what he was saying to me. We looked deep into each other's eyes as we made various love faces. King's dick was hitting a spot that was driving me crazy.

"I want you all to myself. You hear me? You fucking hear me?" he asked as he possessively wrapped his hand around my throat.

I nodded my head in agreement because let's be honest, bomb ass sex would make you sign a pact with the devil.

"I'm gonna cum again," I said as I grabbed a hold of his shoulders.

"Yes, baby, cum for your King." Digging even deeper in my insides, King buried his face at the side of my neck as he exploded inside of me, my own release following his.

As we both breathed loudly trying to recover from our explosive sex, I realized something.

"Shit, King, you said you'd pull out," I said, shoving him by his upper arms.

"I didn't wanna ruin Kwana's sofa." It was only then it hit me that we just fucked once again in his sister's apartment, this time on her sofa.

"We need to stop coming over here. Your sister's apartment is some type of aphrodisiac," I said as we got up and began to get dressed so that he could take my ass home.

Selah

"Yo, I can't come get you later." I paused as I was about to close Lamar's car door.

"The fuck, Lamar, and you only now telling me this? I could have rode my own car over here," I said, wanting nothing more than to hit him upside his big head.

"I now remember I got something to handle this afternoon." I mean mugged Lamar so hard. If I wasn't late for work, I swear I would kick his ass.

"Whatever, stupid!" I yelled at him in a childish manner before I slammed the door in his face and stormed off.

I was fucking late and my asshole boss would be tearing another asshole in my butt as soon as I walked through the front door.

Saying a quick prayer, I eased into the front door and tip-toed over to the reception desk. Jaime was nowhere in sight and I breathed a sigh of relief that he wasn't waiting for me in the front area.

Not even a minute had passed when I powered on my desktop and my work phone rang.

"Shit," I mumbled as Jaime's extension number flashed on the display screen.

"Hello," I said as I made a face, knowing I was about to get reprimanded.

"Are you now getting in?" Jaime asked, his voice making me feel some type of way I couldn't quite explain.

"Um, I got in about ten minutes ago." The lie passed my lips and I bit into my lower lip praying he believed me.

"You're a terrible liar, get in my office," Jaime said as he abruptly hung the phone up in my face.

I groaned softly because I knew he was probably about to give me my first warning. In all fairness, this was the first time in the two weeks I started working that I was late. So Jaime was fucking tripping if he was upset.

Getting off of my chair that didn't even have a chance to get warm yet from me sitting on it, I made my way on over to Jaime's office.

I knocked on the door twice before letting myself in.

Jaime was standing at the front of his desk leaning casually on it, one leg crossed on the other, a hand shoved in his work pants pocket, as he sipped on what I assumed to be a cup of coffee.

Before I go on let me just say this, working for this man had my feelings on a rollercoaster ride. Firstly, I liked my niggas about two shades lighter than Jaime and I would prefer them to also not be a cocky dickhead.

But my nigga Jaime, he made a bitch weak in the knees every single time I was in his presence. His smooth, chocolate brown skin and his arrogant personality made my pussy pulse something wonderful.

I once fantasized about him giving me a pap smear, but instead of using his gynaecology equipment to examine me, he used his mouth and fingers instead. I remember after my little fantasy I had to run into the toilet at the office and wipe myself off from being so wet.

"Yes, Mr. Francis?" I asked as I stood a safe distance away from him as he looked me up and down. Today I wore a simple black and yellow plaid work dress, with a pair of black work pumps. My braids were pulled into a ponytail.

Jaime looked at the expensive watch on his wrist and asked me, "What time did you get in, Selah?" My pussy twitched from the way he said my name.

Exhaling softly, I had no choice but to come clean. "A couple minutes ago," I mumbled under my breath. Jaime shook his arrogant head at me and took a sip of his beverage.

"Only because my first patient is scheduled for ten I won't get in your ass," he said as he placed his cup down on the desk behind him. I chuckled inwardly at what he said.

Jaime, from time to time, would let his street nigga out when he spoke to me. It mostly happened when he got a little upset with me, which would happen at least once every day. It was almost as if I could do nothing right his eyes and he just needed a reason to go off.

I low-key loved when he let those hidden rough-neck ways come out, made me like the fuck out of him even more.

"Can I help you with you something?" I asked since he had yet to let me know why he summoned me in his office in the first place. He raised his eyebrow at me as if to suggest that I had no right to rush him.

"You can actually. I have a conference coming up out of town this weekend." I looked at him puzzled, wondering why he needed to tell me this, since we didn't work on weekends.

"Do you need me to handle your travel arrangements?" I asked him, but he shook his head.

"I already made the airline and hotel reservations for two." I knitted my eyebrows together, not sure why he needed to make reservations for two. Maybe he was taking a girlfriend along or something.

"So, let your little boyfriend know you won't be around this weekend," Jaime said as he picked up his cup and sipped his coffee casually.

My eyes bulged at what he said. He must be joking right? I couldn't go out of town with this man, for more reasons than one. The first being that Lamar still had no idea that I wasn't working for a female as I previously thought.

If he knew my boss was male, and a very fine one at that, he would trip the fuck off, and find ways for me to quit my job.

"Um, why do I have to go?" I asked as I pointed a finger to my chest.

"Because I need you there," Jaime replied curtly as he stared at me.

"There are things that I would need your assistance with. Do you have a problem leaving for the weekend? Your little boyfriend won't sign your permission slip?" he asked with a straight face, and all I wanted to do was throw the remaining contents of what he was drinking in his face.

"Will you be sending me my travel itinerary?" I asked through clenched teeth which only made him smirk at me.

"I already did. I sent it via email. If your ass wasn't late this morning you would have seen it." Deciding that it was time I left his office before I said something that would fuck around and get me fired, I gave Jaime a tight smile preparing to turn around and leave.

As he was about to take another sip of his beverage, he accidentally spilled some on the baby blue shirt he was wearing. I smiled to myself because the universe had found a way to even out the score.

"Fuck," Jaime said as he hurriedly placed the cup back on top of his desk. I stood and watched in silence as he grabbed some napkins from his desk and began rubbing the coffee stain vigorously.

Seeing how he was only making things worse, I went to him and took the napkins from out of his hand. Picking up a water bottle that sat on his desk, I poured a little onto the napkin.

I patted the spot where he spilled the coffee. "If you rub it all you gonna do is make the stain worse, so it's always better that you just pat the area with a little water," I explained to him. I was fully aware of being so close to him and I tried my best to ignore it.

However, the intoxicating scent of his cologne made it hard for me to ignore. What was the name of the scent he was wearing? Was it called fuck me? Because that was all that I wanted to do at that very moment.

I looked up and Jaime was staring down at me in a way that began to make me uncomfortable and very much aware that I was way too close to him. Clearing my throat, I inched away from him handing him the napkins.

"I think it should be good now. I'll just go back to my desk," I said before practically sprinting out of his office.

I sat on my chair and shut my eyes for a couple of seconds. I was supposed to be in a hotel with that nigga for the entire weekend? How the fuck would I be able to keep my hormones in check?

OUR LAST CLIENT for the day was a whole fucking mess, I swear!

Her name was Shantel Cudjoe and she was loud as hell and I couldn't believe what man actually went ahead and got her ass pregnant.

"I'm saying doc. My man is paid and everything, so this baby would never need anything on my life." I rolled my eyes at her, not even caring if she saw me or not as I applied the ultrasound gel to her stomach as I prepared her for her ultrasound.

Jaime would allow me into the examination room with him if it was a simple sonogram procedure. I took a nursing course which was the reason he allowed me to assist him at times.

Jaime had an expression on his face that said he was unimpressed by the way she kept going on and on about her baby's father, who was not here by the way.

"Maybe instead of having a paid baby daddy you should have a responsible one. Since the nigga ain't here," Jaime said. He shocked both me and his patient by his blunt words.

"You ain't gotta be rude doc," she said as she twisted her neck as she spoke. Her blonde, lace-front wig was tied up to the top of her head in a bun, and she came in wearing a dress that was two sizes too small. It was squeezing her little stomach. But she was pretty enough with a rich cinnamon complexion.

"I'm not being rude just honest. Now let's have a look at your bundle of joy here." I stood to the side and tried hard not to laugh at the way Jaime couldn't care less if he was being rude or not.

I watched a little ways off as Jaime passed the wand across her stomach and I saw the peanut shape pop up on the screen. I smiled as I longingly saw how happy Shantel got as she heard her baby's heartbeat.

I secretly wished that one day soon I would be sharing this with that special someone, doubtful that person would be Lamar with his stupid ass.

I suddenly felt as if I was being watched and turned to see that Jaime was staring at me with a curious look on his face. I quickly wiped the smile off my lips and looked away from him.

Jaime began describing to Shantel what she was seeing and told her she was almost three months pregnant. This seemed to excite her even more and she began asking when she would be able to know the sex of her baby.

A half hour after, I was logging off my computer rushing around collecting my belongings so that I could make my way to the bus stop.

I knocked softly on Jaime's door and opened it so that I could tell Jaime I was about to leave.

"Hey, I'm about to head out. I have to catch the bus. I'll see you in the morning at *7:30am*," I told him as I stressed on the time on purpose.

"Hol'up, why you about to take the bus? Your boyfriend took the day off?" he asked as he gathered up his belongings on his desk.

"Na, he can't get me today," I replied as I turned to bolt out the door, not in the mood to miss the bus.

"Let me give you a lift. How can I allow you to catch the bus? I'll be right out." I opened my mouth to protest and let him know I didn't mind catching the bus. But I knew that would have been a lie. I really didn't feel like catching the damn bus.

"Ok, I'll be out front," I told him as I turned and left his office.

I stood waiting outside at the front door biting thoughtfully into my lower lip as I stared at Jaime's ride. Jaime drove a lily-white Audi van; that shit was cold as hell. You could tell he took really good care of his vehicle.

"Let's go," I heard his voice say behind me, causing me to jump a bit. I trailed behind him in silence as he disarmed the car, and I smiled a little as he opened my car door for me, waiting until I was seated to close it and make his way over to the driver's side.

I didn't think Lamar had ever opened a door for me since knowing him, and it felt nice to have someone do that for me.

Looking over at Jaime because he was taking too long to climb inside of the car, I gasped loudly at him standing at his door taking his work shirt off.

What in the world! I thought to myself as my eyes raped his fine ass. He opened the door and got in, clad only in his white vest and I had to force myself to turn my head in the opposite direction.

"I usually take my shirt off before I start driving. I hope you don't mind," he explained as he started his vehicle. I turned to him and licked my lip at the sight of the huge tribal tattoo that stopped just under his elbow and disappeared under his vest.

I wanted nothing more than to remove his vest so that I could see just how big his tattoo was.

"It's ok, I don't mind." *Wait, did I sound thirsty when I said that just then?* I cursed myself in my head, wishing that this ride home would end quickly.

I gave him directions to my home and he entered it in his GPS and we sat in silence... A very strained and uncomfortable silence.

"You checked the itinerary I sent you?" Jaime asked, and I was all too happy to answer because my heart was beating hella loud in my chest.

"Yes, I did. Why are we coming back on Monday though, why not on Sunday?" I asked as I turned to look at him, basically using this as a reason to look at him.

"I tried to get a flight back for Sunday but it was booked. I informed my travel agent to let me know if something opens up though. So it could swing either way." I half listened as I watched how he concentrated on the road. His forehead made these cute creases as he tried to stay focused.

I had to force myself to look away, reminding myself that I was very much a taken woman.

"You and your sister are really different, if you don't mind me saying," I told him, but I was pretty sure he knew this already.

He chuckled softly before answering me. "That's because I'm her adopted brother." My eyes grew wide with shock as I turned to look at him once more.

"You're adopted?" I asked incredulously as he nodded his head at me.

"Actually, technically I'm not, and technically she's really my cousin, but I call her my sister." He must have seen the confused look on my face so he explained himself further. "My mom and I had a very strained relationship. She preferred hanging out in the clubs and partying instead of staying home and being a fucking mother to me.

"One day I came home from school and she was gone like the wind. Packed up all her shit and left. I called up her sister, my auntie Charmaine, and she immediately came over and got me. I'd been in her care since then. Even though she's my aunt, I called her my mom."

"Of course being a young nigga and being abandoned by your own fucking mother could mess with your mental pretty fucking hard, so every chance I got I was getting into trouble. Smoking weed, running the streets selling dope. You name it, I'm pretty sure I did it," he said thoughtfully as he shook his head.

"My aunt, however, refused to give up on me. She stuck by a nigga, made sure I got an education and encouraged me to be a doctor. I'm glad she saw something in me I didn't even see in my own self." The car stopped suddenly and it was only then that I realized we had reached our destination.

I blinked quickly a few times as Jaime and I sat and stared at each other for a few seconds. I fumbled with the door handle as I tore my eyes away from him.

"Thanks so much for giving me a lift home," I said softly, as I smiled his way, pushing the door open.

"I didn't mind at all, thanks for the company." He smiled at me and the walls in my pussy contracted.

I hurriedly climbed out of his vehicle swearing he would figure out just how much he was turning me on.

"I'll see you in the morning for 7:30, Selah."

"Seven thirty it is," I replied as I closed his door.

Jaime gave me one more breath-taking smile before driving off. With shaky legs, I made my way to my front door, wondering how

Jaime was able to have such an effect on me; when I swore he wasn't even my type.

King

wo weeks I'd been working for the Daniels, and I still couldn't stomach the sight of Sammie's husband.

I glanced at him from the rear-view mirror as I drove his ass from his office to his home. The job was cool and all, especially since I got to see Sammie more than once a week; but I knew I wasn't about to do this shit for much longer. I honestly preferred to run the streets.

I knew my mama probably would come in my dreams one day and tell me she was disappointed in me, that I chose to go back to my old ways. But a nigga had to do what he had to in order to survive.

I had my first shipment of some high-grade kush coming in straight from Jamaica shortly. Once I got my niggas to start selling that shit for me and I got my money looking right again, I was about to quit this job.

"Kingsale, I need to make a couple of stops before we get home," Mr. Daniel said as he interrupted my thoughts.

"Aight cool, you'll just direct me," I replied, but in my mind I was cussing his lame ass.

About forty-five minutes later, we stopped in front of a large two-story house. I cut off the engine as Mr. Daniel opened the door at the back and began climbing out.

"I'll be right back," he said as he got out and walked toward the house.

I smiled pensively as I rubbed my chin and looked as he disappeared through the front door. I knew this nigga was getting his bankroll through other means beside being a councillor for his community.

This house that we just rolled up to belonged to none other than Manuel Brixton aka Santa, a notorious drug lord. He got the nickname Santa because he looked like a motherfucking Santa Claus.

He was an over-weight white man with a huge belly, and every Christmas he normally held a turkey and gifts giveaway for the kids in less fortunate areas.

Never mind his nickname was Santa, he was a ruthless motherfucker that would gut you without thinking twice. I personally never dealt with him because I wasn't willing to risk stepping on his corns. Then he would find out the hard way how Jamaicans really got down.

I was curious as fuck, however, on knowing what Sammie's husband was doing messing with Santa. My instincts were telling me that he was no doubt involved in some kind of illegal business. It could run from anything to having his own drug block to money laundering.

I was about to investigate the fuck out of Mr. Daniel to see exactly what he was into.

A few minutes later, the front door opened and Mr. Daniel walked casually out with his hands shoved in his pants pockets.

I started the engine and kept my eyes on him as he made his way to his car. I smiled to myself as the thought of his wife danced in my mind. If this nigga only knew just how much work I was putting down on his wife, he would probably pop a vein in his head.

Sammie and I had fucked twice since the last time we were at my sister's. She had a doctor's appointment and another visit with the realtor within the last couple of weeks. I took her to both destinations then afterward I took her over to my place, so that I could lay this pipe on her.

Now don't get me wrong, it wasn't just about the sex with Sammie;

it was about...Sammie! I knew deep down that I loved her, and I wanted to kidnap her ass and run off with her and live out the remainder of our lives in happiness.

Our slight age difference made Sammie feel as if she was some kind of cougar, but I quickly shut all that noise down when she brought it up. I could give a fuck about our age difference. I was a motherfucking King, in more ways than one. And I planned on making Sammie my Jamaican queen. Her ass just didn't know it yet.

"I got one last stop to make and then you'll take me home," Mr. Daniel requested, and I nodded my head at him. He gave directions to where he needed me to take him and I wondered if this was about to be another drug lord he was about to visit.

"You taking it easy from running around in these streets young nigga?" I creased my eyebrows as I looked at him from the mirror because I was certain he had to be on his phone and not talking to my ass.

"Yeah, I'm trying to stay on the straight and narrow," I replied, and I could literally feel him drilling a hole at the back of my head with his eyes.

"Mmhmm, I heard about you. Heard you had a lot of weight in the streets before you got arrested. I'm a man that wants nothing more than to keep the streets in my community drug free, young nigga." I clenched my jaw at what he said because I knew it was all bullshit; this nigga was a fucking hypocrite.

I would bet my life that he was running out here getting his hands dirty.

"Well I'm out the game, so you won't need to worry about me dirtying your streets, councilman." I kept a stoic expression on my face as I lied, knowing damn well I was about to run the streets again pretty soon.

"Good, good, I'm glad to hear that Kingsale. You can pull up right alongside this house right here." Now I was officially confused because I knew this house. *What the fuck did he want over here?* I thought as I watched him hop out of the car once more.

This day was getting wilder by the minute. I dipped inside of my pocket and pulled out my cell phone and dialled my sister's number. The phone rang off the hook before it took me to voicemail.

I sucked my teeth in annoyance and called her ass again. I had to make a total of four calls before Kwana finally answered.

"What you want King?" she asked as she answered her phone with a funky attitude.

"Why your big-headed ass take so long to answer yo' phone," I fussed at her because she was annoying as hell.

"Boy, don't make me hang this phone up on your stupid ass. What you want?" I sucked my teeth at her before I got to the reason I called her up.

"Listen, that homegirl that came over to your place that one time about a year ago. Shorty who look like she got Indian in her family with the wavy hair," I tried my best to describe Kwana's friend because for the love of me I couldn't remember her name.

"Nigga, who you talking about?" Kwana asked, sounding as if she already had enough of this conversation.

"Focus big head! Remember that one time I came over unannounced and there were two girls over at your place kicking it. One of the chicks was short and light-skinned with that good hair, her hair was long and curly. She had a fat ass and you asked me to take her home and I did," I explained to Kwana as I had my eyes glued on the house because I was certain this was the exact house I dropped shorty off at.

"Oh, you mean, Sandy. She's not really my friend, she just tagged along with Felicia that day. Why are you asking all these questions though?" Kwana asked me.

"Do you know if she still lives the exact same place I dropped her off at?" Kwana clucked her tongue at me and I knew she was about ready to go off.

"Nigga, didn't I just tell your scary ass she not really my friend. Stop trying to encourage me to mind people's business nigga." I was about to tell her shut her stupid ass up, but she hung her phone up on me.

I shook my head at her ignorant ass and shoved my phone back inside of my pocket. I was curious as fuck to know if I was right or not, but turned out I didn't have to wait any longer.

The door opened and my head began bobbing and weaving as I tried to see if anyone was about to walk out with Mr. Daniel. He walked out first and stopped in front of the door but with his back to me.

A female suddenly appeared and excitedly wrapped her arms around his neck. I narrowed my eyes as I focused on the woman and sure enough, it was the same girl, Sandy.

Mr. Daniel looked back at the car with a nervous expression on his face and shoved her back inside the door. It was as if he wanted to make sure that I didn't see the female that he went to visit.

He closed the door quickly before making his way back to the car. He climbed inside of the car and I played it cool even though I knew full well he was creepin' on Sammie.

"My sister is always so happy to see me. You can take me home now." I tried my best not to laugh in his face about that whole sister thing. I started the engine to drive his cheating ass home.

I wasn't even mad he was a wolf in sheep's clothing. All he was doing was making things a whole lot easier to win Sammie over and have her all to myself.

Selah

*T*his had been the best business trip I'd been on. Actually, this had been the only business trip I'd ever been on! And I was enjoying the fuck out of it.

Jaime booked us in a high-end hotel, and our rooms were right opposite each other's, which was cool since we had kept it very professional...well, up until now.

It was Saturday which was the last day of our trip; we would be leaving tomorrow since Jaime ended up getting us on a Sunday flight instead of on Monday. I honestly didn't know why Jaime even wanted me to come along with him.

I didn't have much to do the entire trip. I accompanied him to the conference and wrote down a few minutes of what was being said. I brought him his refreshments while the lecturer spoke about some new type of medical equipment the company was hoping to launch soon.

Presently we were seated in the bar area of the hotel we were accommodating having a few drinks. Our moods were light and relaxed as we talked and got to know one another better.

"So how come you don't have any kids?" I asked him as I took a sip of my mimosa. My head began to get a nice little buzz from the drinks, like two mimosas ago, but whatever.

"Well, I believe I need to have a woman first before I could have kids, right?" Jaime said as he looked at me, his gaze playful as he took a sip of his fourth glass of Hennessy on the rocks.

Jaime wasn't as bad as I thought. Once you got to know him, he was actually a pretty good guy. My eyes roamed lustfully over his face, his full mouth glistening from the alcohol he was drinking.

The plain, baby blue shirt he wore was rolled up to his elbows, which was just the sexiest thing a man could do in my book. The shirt clung to his toned body and all I wanted to do was run my tongue over every inch of his chocolate self until he moaned from the pleasure my tongue gave to him.

I forced myself to look away and focused on my drink instead, feeling like some sort of hoe. Who the fuck fantasizes about their boss any damn way. At least not when he's seated directly opposite them anyway.

"I find it hard to believe that you don't have a woman in your life," I said as I gave him a doubtful look, causing him to chuckle at me.

"Aye, it was a lot of hard work involved in me getting to where I'm at today. Most females I came across didn't want a man who was chasing his dreams; they wanted one who already had their shit together." He shrugged his shoulders as he looked at the watch on his wrists.

"How about you? How long have you been with your nigga?" Sometimes it was hard to think of Jaime as my boss when he spoke so street. I knew more about his background now, so I got that he still had a little street nigga in him... And we all knew just how much I appreciated a street nigga.

"Only a few months," I replied as my mind went to Lamar. Just the thought of him and the fact that he still had no idea my boss was actually a man and not the woman he thought hired me, had me feeling kind of bad for not being totally honest with him.

He was of the belief that I was on this business trip with my female boss and not a fine nigga who made my pussy leak every time he was next me. I promised myself that when I got back home that I would let him know the truth, and I knew he would breathe fire up my ass when I did.

"I hope he treats you like nothing less than a queen," Jaime said as he focused on me intently, his eyes glued on my lips.

"Well, you know every relationship has its ups and downs, but I guess he treats me good," I said as Jaime and I were now staring at each other, making my breathing pattern become difficult.

I wasn't quite sure if it was the alcohol or the way Jaime was looking at me that caused my body to feel warm all over. But my entire body felt as though it was on fire.

"Maybe it's time we went back to our rooms; it's almost midnight," Jaime said, finally forcing us to look away from each other. Nodding my head in agreement, I gathered up my purse as we stood to make our way to the elevator.

The ride up to our rooms in that elevator was the longest few seconds of my life. We stood next to each other, close enough that I felt his body heat emanating from off him. I kept my eyes on the moving numbers, finding the elevator was taking way too fucking long to get to our floor.

I didn't know if it was my imagination or not, but I swore I felt Jaime's eyes on me the entire elevator ride. When those doors finally opened I almost tripped over my damn feet trying to get out of there as fast as I could.

"Do you need a wake-up call in the morning so that you won't over sleep?" Jaime asked me, seeing that our flight was for seven and we needed to be at the airport two hours before that.

"Na, I normally don't have any issues waking up," I said as I took my room key out and swiped it, hearing the loud click. I turned to Jaime who already had his door open and was looking back at me.

"Well, have a good night, I'll see you in the morning." It was crazy the way we were looking at each other, but I had to keep telling myself that I could not fuck my boss right about now; nothing good could come out of that.

"Night, Selah," Jaime said as he gave me one final look before turning to walk into his room. I did the same, closing the door behind me. I leaned back on the cold, wooden door and exhaled loudly.

I placed a hand between my legs because my pussy was pulsing so much it hurt.

"Shit," I mumbled in frustration as I got undressed to take my horny ass into the shower.

About fifteen minutes later I was wrapped in the hotel robe as I attempted for like the fifth time to zip my luggage after I was done packing, but the stupid zipper was stuck.

I tugged at it one final time and then groaned in frustration. I tugged at my braids that were in a bun at the top of my head, allowing the strands to fall down to my shoulders.

I bit into my lower lip and wondered if Jaime would mind coming to assist me. Looking at the small radio on the nightstand, it was almost one in the morning. I grabbed my cell from off the bed and dialled Jaime's number, and he picked up on the second ring.

"I didn't wake you, did I?" I asked, as I waited for his reply.

"Na, I just got out the shower. What's up?" Visions of Jaime standing with a towel wrapped around his waist played in my head, until I had to literally shake my head to get the image out.

"I was packing but my zipper got stuck. My girlie strength is unable to free it, so do you mind coming over to assist me?" I asked.

"Yeah, just gimme five minutes," he said to me before ending the call.

Less than five minutes after, there was a soft knock at the door. I looked down at myself thinking I should have changed from out my robe.

I walked over and opened the door and almost shut that shit in Jaime's face. He was wearing grey sweatpants and a black vest, and his body looked like sin itself. His tribal tattoo made him look even sexier.

"Um, co-come in," I stuttered, as I moved to one side to allow him to walk past me.

Jaime walked to the bed where the luggage was and after about three tries he was able to free the stuck zipper. He removed the luggage from off the bed and placed it on the floor then stood up and looked at me.

"My hero," I joked as I turned to walk him out. As I stood in front of the door about to open it, I felt his body press gently into mine. I held my breath as my hand paused on the door handle.

"You're driving a nigga crazy, you know that," I heard Jaime say into my ear. I shut my eyes as I felt his hand travel up my sides all the while a voice in my head screamed that this wasn't right.

"Jaime, we can't do this; you're my boss," I said barely above a whisper as his hands palmed my ass through my robe.

"You want me to stop?" he asked as he wrapped his hand around my braids, forcing my head back as his lips kissed the side of my neck, stopping to nibble on my skin. "I've been wanting to tug on these damn braids since the first day you walked into my office," he confessed to me.

"Mmmm," was my only response as his tongue tasted my skin. Jaime reached to the front of me and slowly untied my robe, opening it, exposing my naked body. He pulled the robe down my shoulders, dropping it to the floor around my ankles.

I stood naked as Jaime said in my ear, "Turn around for me, Selah." I complied to his wishes as I spun around to face him. His eyes took me all in as he licked his lips as if I were a meal he was about to devour.

"I promise this won't change our work relationship, but I really do like you, Selah. From the moment you walked through my office door I couldn't keep my eyes off you," Jaime said as his hands began roaming boldly over my curves.

I would have never thought Jaime felt that way about me, seeing how he was always such a cocky asshole, like ninety percent of the time.

"I don't know, Jaime I think no good would come out of this." I bit into my lower lip as Jaime's fingers found my breasts and his index finger made circles around my nipples.

"Let's focus on the now and worry about the after later on." Before

I could even protest again, Jaime dipped his head and enclosed his mouth on my left nipple.

"Shit," I gasped out in pleasure at the way his mouth felt so warm against my skin. I thrust my body forward, encouraging him on as I placed my hand to the back of his head. I would worry about how shitty of an idea this was later.

Removing his mouth, he roughly kissed my lips as I eagerly wrapped my arms around his neck. Our tongues played with each other's then Jaime lifted me bodily from under my ass.

I yelped out in surprise and instinctively wrapped my legs around his waist. I stuck my tongue out at him and he quickly placed the pink tip into his mouth and sucked on it seductively as he walked us over to the bed.

His rock-hard erection pressed into my stomach and I couldn't wait to feel him inside of me. Gently, he laid me down on the bed, never breaking our kiss. I felt his hand run between my thighs getting closer to my centre that had been aching for him the past couple of weeks.

"Jaime," I said as I moaned his name against his lips. I opened my legs even wider as Jaime's fingers circled my clit at a fast pace.

"Acting like you didn't want this and this pussy so wet for a nigga," Jaime said as he removed his mouth from mine so he could look at my face as his fingers drove me insane.

"Shit, Jaime." I squeezed my eyes shut as he replaced his fingers with his mouth. I grasped his shoulders as his mouth devoured me hungrily, his lips plucked tenderly at my clit as he groaned.

Placing his tongue at my opening, he began thrusting it in and out of me. I dug my nails into Jaime's shoulders as I lifted my ass from off the bed, my hips matching the movement of his tongue.

"Yeah baby, fuck my face." With his dirty talk and the way his tongue was working me over, I began feeling my orgasm building. My body tensed as my nails dug into his shoulders even harder as my release hit me like a ton of bricks.

"Oh my goddddd!" I screamed out as my body convulsed uncontrollably. I breathed loudly as I tried to calm down, and Jaime gave my pussy one last kiss before he stood up.

Now standing before me, he looked down at me with a sly smile on his lips. Holding his vest, he pulled it over his head and tossed it on the bed next to me. I was finally allowed to see the body I'd been fantasizing about and I was not disappointed.

His chest was well chiselled. I looked in awe at the tribal tattoo covering his entire left chest, his biceps were nice and firm and well defined, and his abdominals were perfectly sculpted. This man was nothing short of a work of art and he wasn't even completely naked yet.

As he held my gaze, he slowly inched his sweatpants down his waist and then his hips, his dick springing out as if it were happy to finally be free.

I eyed his dick with uncertainty, not sure if I would be able to take his massive length and girth that was filled with big, juicy veins. I was low-key mad most of the mimosas I had consumed earlier weren't in my system as much as before. I think I needed to be inebriated to take all of his length.

"Wait," I said as he climbed on top of me using his knee to push one of my legs further apart. He paused and looked down at me with a perplexed look on his face.

"A condom, do you have one?" I understood I was being a pussy right now by trying to stall him. But that was because I was trying to save my pussy from being killed at this very moment.

"I get tested every six months, I'm good. What 'bout you?" he asked as he used the tip of his dick to tease the inside of my slit, stopping to tap my clit with the head of his dick.

"I got tested a few months ago...uughhh," I moaned as Jaime began entering me slowly. He took his time as the walls of my pussy stretched out to accommodate his size.

"Jaime," I moaned out his name as he was now entirely inside of me. As his strokes began picking up the pace, my body adjusted to him.

As he balanced his body weight on the palms of his hands, I looked up at him, biting down on my lower lip as Jaime pumped savagely inside of me.

"Open even wider for me baby," Jaime requested, and I did what he asked by wrapping my hand from under my upper thigh, holding my leg further apart.

"Yeah, that's it," he said as he continued ramming his dick inside of me. This allowed me to feel every, single stroke he gave even more, hitting a spot…that spot. The spot that made a bitch speak in tongues.

"Shit, right there…right there, baby. Don't stop," I begged as my eyes began to water because of the ecstasy his strokes were giving to my pussy. A bitch was about to go ape shit in this motherfucking hotel room.

"You like that?" I nodded my head in response as I made whimpering noises, unable to talk because I knew I was about to cum again.

"What's my name, Selah?"

"Jaime."

"What's my name, Selah?" he repeated his question as I began panting loudly and his pumps grew faster.

"Jaimeeee," I groaned louder as I grabbed my breasts and squeezed them.

"Aye, hold that motherfuckin' leg up," he demanded of me, and I had no choice but to listen.

"Who's fucking you, Selah?" He wrapped a hand around my neck this time and squeezed gently.

"Jaime…Jaime's fucking this pussy." As soon as I said that shit, I came so fucking hard I damn near passed the fuck out.

"Yeah, baby I felt that shit," he said, before his own release came, slamming his body viciously into mine.

"Oh fuckkkkkk," he groaned out as he exploded…inside of me.

"Shit, Jaime, don't buss inside me," I argued as I pushed against his chest. But it was entirely too late because I felt his warm liquid enter my body.

"Sorry, I couldn't stop baby. You felt fucking amazing." He kissed the tip of my nose as he gazed down at me. I smiled at him and he smiled back at me.

Well, this would not end well. I felt that shit in the depths of my soul. I just cheated on Lamar and what made me feel twenty times worse was the fact that I enjoyed every lick, every suck and every thrust that Jaime gave me.

"Hey," Jaime said as he held me under my chin, and I gave him a nervous smile.

"I meant what I said; this won't affect our work relationship. If you want this to be a one-time thing I'd completely understand. I just want you to know that this wasn't just a sex thing for me. I like you." My chest constricted at his words and I tenderly kissed his lips.

"I like you too. Stay the rest of the night with me." He nodded his head and shifted his body weight off me so that he was now laying on his side. He wrapped his arm possessively around me and before I knew it, he fell asleep, snoring softly.

I looked at his face and how peaceful he looked when he slept. What was I going to do? I got myself into a hell of a situation.

Jaime was everything I never knew I wanted.

Samantha

"Skin up this *pum pum* for me, baby." *Jesus, King's dirty talk during sex was on a different level every time.* I opened my legs further apart for him, since I knew that was what he wanted.

"Yeah, just like that," King groaned as he drilled into me even more. So here was my hoe ass, getting fucked for like the fourth time this week. I'd been finding every excuse in the book to leave the house since King was hired.

I said anything that I could think of; all of a sudden, I was one busy bitch. I always had some type of errand to run and I always needed King to take me on them. All the while we would end up over at his house just so he could screw my brains out.

Exactly what was happening at the moment.

"Oh shit, baby," I moaned as I placed my hand on his hip as I tried to get him to slow down his pumps. But all that got me was a slap on my wrist, tossing my hand away.

"Aw, shit. Backshot position baby," King said as he pulled out of me. I knew now what position he meant, but the first time he used that phrase I was confused as hell. Until he told me it meant the doggie pose.

I turned around quickly and got on my knees. King placed his palm in the middle of my back forcing my body further down. I closed my eyes and sucked in my lower lip as I felt him place his tip at my opening.

"You about to throw it back for me?" he asked softly as he entered me slowly, sucking in his breath as he did so. I grabbed the sheet on the bed and bunched it up in my hands.

Slap!

King slapped my ass hard, and I whipped my head around to look at him.

"You ain't hear me ask you a question? You about to throw it back on your King?" he repeated his question as he picked up his pace.

Not bothering to answer his question because action spoke louder than words, I placed my forehead on the mattress and began bouncing my ass back against him.

"Sssssssss, yeah baby," King hissed as he enjoyed the ride I was giving his ass.

"Do you think maybe we should start using condoms?" I asked him about twenty minutes after getting out his shower and getting dressed so that he could take me home.

"For fucking what, Sammie? We ain't never used them before. Why, you trying to tell me something? You fucking somebody else?" He came up to me and grabbed my upper arm. I looked at him and shook my head because he was so jealous at times.

Sometimes I swore he forgot that I was a very much married woman. But I had reassured him that Adam hadn't touched me in months.

"No, I'm not sleeping with anyone else, King," I said as I pulled out of his hold. "I'm just saying, I'm still a married woman and you haven't exactly been careful in the pull-out department lately." I scolded him because his pull-out game had been weak as fuck lately. The last thing I needed was to end up pregnant because there was no doubt that King would be the father. Seeing that Adam and I hadn't had sex in forever. Not that I cared either way.

I buttoned my skinny jeans as I kept an eye on his face to see his expression. He said nothing as he buttoned his work shirt as he avoided looking in my direction.

"King, I know you aren't purposely bussin' in me." Silence in the motherfucking house as he casually looked over in my direction as I gasped in shock. "Kingsale Rock," I said, using his full government name as I marched over to where he stood and folded my arms angrily in front of me as I glowered at him.

"What you want me to say Sammie?" he asked as he spread his arms wide with a stupid look on his face. "Think I don't know you want to have a baby? I see the way you get hearts in your eyes when you are around my nephew," he replied as he looked down at me.

I couldn't argue with what he said. Being around his nephew had my baby fever even worse. But there was nothing I could do about it. I began thinking that for some reason I just couldn't conceive.

"King, that isn't your call to make. You know I'm married. How am I gonna explain a baby to my husband when we don't even have sex?" I asked, and all that got me was him sucking his teeth loudly at me.

"Yo, I'm not tryna hear nothing 'bout your *batty boy* husband," he said as he walked off on me to go sit on his bed as he put his shoes on. "And if you get pregnant, so what. I'll be there for my baby and you'll just get a divorce. Don't see why you still with that fuck nigga anyway," he mumbled under his breath.

"King, do you hear yourself? All those things are easier said than done. If I turn up pregnant there's no way I could keep the baby. I—"

Giving me no time to complete my sentence, King pounced off the bed and within the blink of an eye he was in my face.

"What you saying? Huh, if you get pregnant with my baby you'll have an abortion? Huh, Sammie?" he asked as he grabbed my face, roughly squeezing my cheeks in until it hurt.

"King, I mean, I'm married and you're younger than me. I don't even see any other way." King shut his eyes tightly as he tried to process my words. He removed his hand from off my face.

As he opened his eyes to look at me, they were icy cold and filled with rage.

"I'm too young now? A few minutes ago you were begging for this young dick." I felt my face grow hot with embarrassment and turned to walk away from him.

Grabbing my wrist, he spun me back around to face him as he pointed his index finger in my face almost poking my eye out.

"I promise you, if you get pregnant and get rid of my baby, just so your *pussyhole* husband doesn't find out, I'll show you how a real Jamaican shotta does it." His words and glare were very intimidating, so much that for the first time I was a little scared of him.

Saying nothing more, he stormed out of his bedroom slamming the door behind him, leaving me standing there alone. I sighed softly and sat down on his bed.

I twisted my fingers nervously on my lap contemplating on if I should go find King. I decided that I should just leave him to cool off on his own.

I sighed again, thinking that I had gotten myself in a hell of a dilemma. I knew King cared deeply for me. He didn't have to say it; I could tell. I could tell by the little things he did, the way he would always have Hershey kisses chocolates in the car because he knew how much I loved them.

The way he always made sure to ask me if I ate whenever I was in his presence.

He even started opening the car door for me, which I swear was the sweetest thing ever. I smiled to myself because even though I knew he cared for me, the feeling was very much mutual. I cared about King so much that I always looked forward to seeing him.

And the sex that we were having was off the chain; it felt as though we just couldn't get enough of each other. But I knew what we were doing was wrong and I knew my ways would catch up with me eventually.

Did I see myself making a new life with King? There were days when I did, when I would think fuck it; we should just run off and be with each other. Then there were the days when I would find a million and five excuses as to why it wouldn't work.

I sat on that bed for a few minutes alone with my thoughts until King walked back into the room with an envelope in his hand. We looked at one another as if we were waiting to see who would be the first person to speak up.

"I'm sorry," we both said simultaneously, making us both laugh. I walked to where he stood and we embraced each other tightly. He bent and pecked me on my lips as he handed me the envelope.

Curiosity formed on my face as I looked down at the large, brown envelope in my hand.

"What's this?" I asked him as I knitted my brow as I inspected the envelope.

"Happy birthday," he replied, causing me to laugh loudly because it wasn't even my birthday today. I walked back over to the bed and sat down.

"You are so silly, but really, what is it?" I turned the envelope around a couple of times as I tried to figure out what was inside. I squeezed it and it felt like paper of some sort.

"Would you just go on ahead and open it up," King said as he laughed at the way I was inspecting the envelope.

Shrugging my shoulders in a dramatic fashion, I tore open the envelope and peeked inside, and I gasped as I did so. Turning the envelope upside down, a wad of money fell on the bed and I looked up at King wondering why in the hell was he giving me all this cash.

"What is this?" I asked as I picked up a stash that was held together by rubber bands.

"That's to help you purchase your yoga studio." I looked up at him stunned as he smiled down at me.

"King, oh my god. I can't accept this," I told him as I eyed the money that I knew I needed, but I just couldn't accept it.

"The fuck you mean you can't accept it? What type of man would I be if I knew you desired something and I knew damn well I could help you get it, but didn't. I'm gon' help you get that shit. I saw how yoga makes you happy and want to help you achieve your goal. So fuck all that you can't accept it bullshit." I looked at him for a couple of seconds before staring at the money again.

I knew King was hard-headed and he would have never allowed me to give the money back to him. I placed the money back inside of the envelope and placed it on my lap as I watched it in silence.

"I'll pay you back one day, I promise," I said as I looked up at him with sincere eyes. It was the least I could do because King didn't have to offer this to me.

"Did I ask your stupid ass to pay me back? Come on; let's bounce." I rolled my eyes at him because his smart mouth was too much sometimes. I got up to gather up my belongings so that he could take me home. I shoved the envelope of money in my Louis Vuitton handbag and walked to where king stood with his hand outstretched to me.

I smiled at him as I took his hand in mine and we walked out of his home hand in hand as if we were long time lovers.

I was all smiles as I hopped out of the shower about two hours after King dropped me off at home. I was super excited to give my real estate agent a call and let her know I would be able to take the spot after all.

I smiled as I towel dried myself, thinking about how thoughtful King was for giving me the balance that I required. I swear King was like some sort of knight in shining armour that came crashing into my life.

He showed me so much of what I needed in my life. The attention he spoiled me with, the way he knew exactly how to bring to life both my body and my mind; I really appreciated him.

I turned to walk to the bed and I almost caught a heart attack at the sight of Adam leaning casually on the frame of the door looking at me.

"Jesus!" I exclaimed as I placed a hand on my chest as I clutched the towel around my naked body. "You scared me, Adam. When did you get home? I didn't hear you come in," I said as I walked to the bed, grabbing up my body lotion and began applying it to my body.

"You seem to be in a good mood." I turned to him confused by what he said as he stood staring at me.

"What? What you mean by that?" I asked as he strolled slowly into the room coming to stand in front of me. He had a weird expression on his face and my hands slowed down a bit from rubbing the lotion on my arms.

"You smiling to yourself, humming and shit. You didn't even realize I was standing here looking at you." I tried my best not to let my face show that I was shocked at what he said. Was I really humming? Did I have a smile on my face as I thought about King?

Being unfaithful was something I never, ever had done in my entire marriage. So it was no surprise that I was acting out of character and I really couldn't afford for Adam to find out I was cheating on him with King.

"I didn't even know I was smiling. I was just thinking of something that Selah told me earlier when we spoke on the phone," I lied to him, but of course I was always an awful liar, so he saw straight through my bullshit.

"You were always such a terrible fucking liar, wife," he said, and I took a step back from him. Whenever Adam called me wife it was a way of me knowing that he was really upset.

I swallowed nervously as he closed the space in between us and grabbed me by my face harshly, squeezing my cheeks in.

"Let me find out you cheating on me, Samantha." I couldn't help the giggle that passed my lips as I laughed in his face like a lunatic.

"Did I say something funny to you?" he asked, and I could tell he was pissed, but I couldn't care less because he had some nerve.

I wriggled my face out of his death grip and for once, I stood my ground. "You have a lot of nerve Adam, accusing me of cheating on you when you couldn't even keep it in your pants one day after we were married. You think everyone is like you? Just running around screwing everybody." He narrowed his eyes at me in disbelief, as if he couldn't believe I had the balls to speak to him in such a manner.

"Oh, that nigga got you feeling yourself, huh? Got you thinking you could talk down to your husband." His upper lip sneered in a menacing way and I knew from here on out I had to tread lightly.

"Nobody's cheating on you, Adam. So you could just stop with all your accusations," I told him as I looked him in his eyes trying my utmost best not to allow my facial expression to let him know I was lying.

His eyes travelled from the tips of my toes to the top of my head slowly, and before I could stop him he snatched the towel from around me. I gasped loudly in shock as I tried to take it back from his hand.

I stood as still as I could as his eyes roamed over my body. I said a silent prayer in my head that King didn't leave any of his love bites on my body. He had done so a couple of times and I had to pull him up on it.

I looked at my husband as he inspected my body, making a complete circle around my naked form. I was so nervous I could barely breath as Adam and I were once again face to face.

Tossing the towel back at me, allowing it to hit me in my face, Adam seemed satisfied with his invasion of privacy.

"You know better than to cross me right, baby?" he asked as he bent to me, bringing his lips closer to mine. I held my breath again thinking he was about to kiss me.

Whoop!

With absolutely no warning, this maniac head butted my ass. Let me say this, I saw all the nine planets with that shit. I'm talking about, Mars, Uranus and them other bitches.

"Uugghhhh, shit…ouch!" I groaned softly as I lifted my hand to tenderly touch the spot Adam hit on my forehead.

"Don't you think you could double cross me, you *my* wife!" he shouted at me before turning to quickly leave the room.

Tears formed in my eyes as my vision began getting flashes of multi-color lights in them. I walked slowly to the bed and crawled into it. I took my time as I laid down on the cool sheets, completely naked.

I held on to my bruised forehead as I crouched my body in a fetal position.

I stayed my ass in that spot in so much pain that I couldn't even think straight. With tears wetting the pillowcase that I laid on, I welcomed the sleep that took over me within a few minutes.

Selah

I'd never felt so guilty about getting some dick in my entire life. I could barley look at Lamar when I got back home. Guilt was eating my ass from the inside out.

Even though I felt guilty for cheating, it was worth every sweat that dripped from my body, every orgasm that Jaime gave me. I'd never had my body handled the way Jaime took care of it that night.

Before we left to go to the airport we went at it again and if it was even possible, that time was even better than the first. Jaime may not have looked as if he wasn't about the hood life, but the way that nigga put it down in the bedroom, I felt the bad boy in him with every stroke he delivered and every dirty word he said in my ear.

And now that we were back in the office, I had no idea how to fucking act. I was tripping over my feet when we were in the same room, avoiding eye contact with Jaime whenever we spoke face to face.

I knew he said we could go back to normal and he wouldn't treat me any differently after we had sex. But how the fuck was I supposed to go about my day when this nigga looked and smelled so good. Everything about him had me all in my feelings. I wanted him to call me in his examining room and lay me on top of his examining table and do all the freaky shit he did to me back on our business trip.

He had just gotten done attending to his last patient for the day and I couldn't wait to go home. I powered off my desktop and grabbed up my car keys from off the desk because I drove myself here, not wanting to put my faith in Lamar again.

With my belongings in hand I stood outside Jaime's office door taking a couple deep breaths before I knocked, to let him know I was about to leave. Thinking that I had finally steadied my nerves, I raised my hand and prepared to knock on his door.

Before I did, the door suddenly burst open and Jaime bumped right into me almost knocking my ass to the floor.

"Shit," he said as he grabbed hold of my upper arms as I stumbled back. "I'm so sorry Selah, I had no idea you were standing behind the door."

We remained pressed up against each other even though it was more than safe for him to let go of me.

"Um, I was just coming in to let you know I was leaving," I said, my voice barely audible, as Jaime and I stood mushed together looking into each other's eyes.

"Ok, I'll be leaving in a little bit too." I gave him a weak smile as I pulled away from him and turned to leave. Not even making two steps, I felt Jaime's hand wrap around my wrist. I closed my eyes as my body instantly reacted to his touch.

"Hey," he said, and I turned around once again to face him. "You good? I kind of feel as though you've been avoiding me all day."

You damn right I've been avoiding your ass, I thought to myself. But of course I didn't say that. "Avoiding you? Why do you think that? I wasn't avoiding you," my untruthful ass said to him as I looked him dead in his eyes.

He gave me a look as if to say, *yeah right.* "I told you, what happened between us wouldn't affect our work relationship. If you want it to be a one-time thing I'll understand and respect your wishes," Jaime said as he stepped closer to me.

My heart began pounding loudly in my chest, so much I swore it would burst through my rib cage. Jaime lifted his hand and caressed my cheek as we gazed into each other's eyes.

"I don't mind us being a constant thing though," he said, right before I felt his lips on mine. I moaned as I opened my mouth allowing his tongue to invade the inside of my mouth.

I wrapped my arms around his neck as Jaime's hand held on to the end of my ponytail and tugged on it roughly. Before I knew it, Jaime had turned me around and had me pressed up on the wall as he palmed my breasts through the thin material of my shirt.

"I can't get enough of you, you know that," he said, as I felt his hand under my skirt running up my inner thigh; as it made its way to the outside of my underwear.

"Uh, fuck," I said as I gasped when I felt his fingers rubbing on me through my panties. Prying his lips away from mine, Jaime and I stared at each other as his fingers rubbed on my pussy.

"This juicy pussy," he whispered as his fingers shifted my underwear to one side and dived inside of my slippery slit.

I was panting loudly like a dehydrated Doberman as Jaime effortlessly drove my body close to the edge with his fingers.

A sudden ringing in his pants pocket forced me back to my senses. *What the fuck was I doing?* I had a whole nigga at home and here I was allowing my boss to finger fuck my horny ass.

"Stop, Jaime," I said as I reached between us and held on to his hand and began pushing it away. He immediately removed his hand from me, an apologetic look on his face.

"I'm sorry," he said as he reached for his ringing cell phone in his pants pocket.

"No, I'm sorry. I got a man and you're my boss; this is wrong. I definitely think what happened back at the hotel should be nothing more than a one-time thing. I'll see you in the morning." Not even giving him a chance to reply to me, I pushed past him and bolted out the front door.

Once outside, I breathed a sigh of relief mixed with frustration as I made my way to my car and unlocked the door and hopped in.

"Jesus," I sighed as I ran my hands through my braided ponytail. Between my thighs felt wet as hell. Grabbing up my handbag I fished around inside and found a small pack of wipes.

Without an ounce of shame, I opened my legs and wiped myself off as best as I could. Tossing the used wipe in my handbag and taking out my cell phone, I decided I needed to talk to my sister.

"Hey, Selah," she said, answering on the second ring.

I smiled hearing her voice. Feeling as though this phone call wasn't enough, I had to go see her.

"What's good, sis? You home?" I asked as I started up my ride and pulled out of the parking lot waiting on her reply.

"Yeah I'm home, what's up?"

"I'm finna come see you." Not even waiting for her to reply, I abruptly ended the call. I needed to clear my head and I believed a sister to sister one-on-one was just what I needed.

"I hoped you cooked; a bitch is starving," I said as I walked inside my sister's home, following her as she walked in the direction of her kitchen.

"Why you ain't eat before you came over here? Always eating up all my food whenever you come through," she fussed, but she went to make me a plate anyway. Between the both of us, Sammie was the one who handled herself well in the kitchen. I could cook, but let's just say I wasn't the best at it.

I took a seat at the island that sat in the middle of her kitchen and observed her in silence. There was something different about her, but I couldn't quite put my finger on it.

"How was your business trip?" she asked as she placed a plate of vegetable rice and fried chicken in front of me. I began eating, knowing I had to confess to somebody that I slept with my boss.

"Girl, I slept with my boss on our trip," I said as I confided in her, shoving the chicken in my mouth. Sammie's mouth dropped open and I groaned as I nodded my head at her.

"Wait, hold up; didn't you say your boss was a female?" she said as she tilted her head to one side as she gave me a sceptical look.

I quickly explained to her about Jaime and Sharon and the office they shared.

"Selah, so what are you going to do? Continue sleeping with him? You better hope Lamar don't find out about it." I groaned again at the sound of Lamar's name because he would kill my ass if he found out I was cheating on him.

"Girl, he still thinks my boss is a female. I mean, technically she is, it's just she's not there at the moment. So really, I didn't lie to him... right?" Sammie gave me a look letting me know I was on some bullshit.

"What do you think I should do? I swear Sammie, the sex was so good." I closed my eyes briefly as thoughts about what Jaime did to my body floated in my head. "I'm not sure if I could stay working there and not want him in that way."

"Girl, you asking the wrong one for advice. Me and King have been humping like rabbits." I dropped the fork and it fell with a loud clinking sound on the plate.

"Bitch, what! You still fucking King, how are you even pulling that off?" I asked, still in shock that my goody two shoes sister had it in her to be an unfaithful wife.

"Remember I told you he replaced his uncle as our driver. I've been lying to Adam about my whereabouts just so I could spend most of my time with King." I couldn't help the wide smile that spread across my face. Sammie and I were truly sisters. We were even cheating on our men at the same damn time.

As I looked at her, I noticed a small black and blue spot on her forehead and I creased my eyebrows in curiosity. She noticed that I was staring at the bump and tried to cover it, bringing her hair down onto her face.

I immediately smacked her hand away. "The fuck is that, Sammie? Who did that, was it Adam?" I asked as I reached up and tenderly touched her bruised skin.

"It's nothing really," she said as she tried to play it off. However, I wasn't about to hear that *it's nothing really shit.*

"Sammie, I thought you said a while back that he stopped putting his hands on you," I said to her, mad that her husband was the one doing all his dirt and still had the nerve to put his hands on my sister.

I knew about Adam's abusive ways, which was one of the reasons I didn't like his ass. He was a cheating and occasionally abusive husband to my family. I just wished Sammie would get the courage to leave him one day.

"He suspected that I may be sleeping with someone else." *The audacity of that dick head!* He cheated on my sister so many times, I was certain even he lost track.

"Fuck Adam, Sammie. That nigga stay cheating on you and the one time you step out and get some dick, he does that to you," I said as I pointed to the mark on her head.

"Is King worth it? All this sneaking around that you doing, I can see you glowing and shit," I said, and she looked over at me and gave me the biggest smile, and I knew her ass was sprung.

"The dick's that good huh?" I asked her, and we both burst into laughter when she nodded her head vigorously in response.

"I know that's right," I said as we both raised our glasses of orange juice at each other taking a sip.

"So now what?" Sammie asked as we looked at each other. I shrugged my shoulders, not knowing how to answer her question because I really liked Jaime. He was different from what I was used to.

And I could tell that King had my sister's nose all the way the open, even though he was a few years younger than her. He was making her happy and I could tell.

"There's something else I didn't tell you," Sammie said as she played with her fingers.

"What's that?" I asked her.

"Remember I told you I wanted to open up my own yoga studio?" I nodded my head because Sammie took that up a couple years ago and she seemed to really enjoy it. "Well I was short by $10,000 and King gave it to me."

My eyes grew a full three sizes bigger. "Are you serious right now?" I asked as I looked at her with a shocked expression on my face.

"He did. I swear he acts way older than his age, Selah. He makes me feel as if I'm the only woman in the world," she gushed as she spoke about her side piece. But I could tell he was way more than a side piece to her; she looked as though she had fallen hard for that man.

"Girl, you got that good, good, having niggas giving you a whole stash like that," I said as I gave her a high five as we both giggled.

"Do you like Jaime?" she asked me, and I got serious as I nodded my head in response. "And he's not even a hustler. I knew you could do it," Sammie cracked as she burst out laughing.

"Shut up, Sammie."

"Nah, but I think you should go on ahead and give that man a try. Forget Lamar's cheating ass; maybe Jaime would be the one for you. So what if he's your boss. If he's cool with it, I say do you boo," she told me, as she playfully bounced our shoulders together.

"Only if you give King a fair chance." The smile instantly wiped off her face and I sucked my teeth in annoyance because she was such a fucking chicken.

"Really, Sammie. I could tell you like the fuck out that nigga so what the problem is?" I asked her.

"You know my situation is not that simple, Selah. I'm a married woman." I rolled my eyes at what she said.

"You're a married woman to somebody who cheats on you with white bitches and knocks you around occasionally. Stop being a door mat for that fool." She got real quiet and I decided to stop pressing her on the issue.

We sat in silence as I finished my meal, both of us lost in our own thoughts no doubt. I got up and cleared my dishes taking them to the sink, and Sammie walked with me.

"Hey," Sammie said, placing her hand on my arm. I turned to look at her and she smiled warmly at me. "I love you big sis," she said, as she reached in and hugged me.

"I love you too girl. How can I not love you when we both cheating on our niggas?" We both fell out laughing as she helped me with the dishes.

King

"The infamous Kingsale Rock, so we finally meet," Manuel Brixton said as he walked up to me with his hand outstretched so that I could shake it.

I shoved the hoodie off the top of my head as I stood up from off the chair to greet the man known as Santa in the drug world.

I know I said before I never fucked with this nigga on this level before, but I had my reasons for what I was about to do. I got my shipment of high-grade marijuana from my homeland Jamaica a few days ago and I needed a buyer for it.

The street value of the weed was close to 500k. I wanted to try something new for once. Instead of distributing my product I wanted to sell my entire weight to one person. So that's where this fool Santa was about to come in.

"What's good, Santa," I said as I tried not to stare at him too much as we shook each other's hand. The nickname Santa suited him perfectly. This motherfucker was wider than the whole of outside with a big ass beer belly. I bet the last time this fool saw his dick was the Summer of '83.

"What you got for me?" he asked as he pointed to the sofa, letting me know to have a seat.

We sat down and I wasted no time to get to the point. "I heard you were the man I should talk to with respects to my product," I explained as he looked at me intently. I took a quick scan of the room wondering where his henchmen were because I knew he wasn't about to do a drug transaction without proper security.

"My men are around; I see you looking. If you try any sneaky shit they'll be on you like white on rice." I smiled at him. I liked the way he did he business. I desired to be like him one day.

"Cool, cool, I feel you," I said with a cool nod of my head.

"What type of product are you looking to move?" he asked me.

"I got that good, high-grade Jamaican kush. You ain't about to get what I have anywhere else." I could brag about my product because I knew it was the best. One pull from a blunt supplied from me and a nigga would be up in the clouds in record time.

"You got any on you for me to see what the hype is about?" I smiled at him and nodded my head. I dipped in my jeans pocket and pulled out a small foil packet and handed it over to him.

I sat and watched in silence as he unwrapped the foil and inspected the marijuana tucked inside. He pulled it apart and ran his fingers through it before putting it up to his nose and inhaling the aroma.

"How much of this you got?" he asked me, and I smiled knowing I had him right where I wanted him.

"How much of that good grade you want? Let's talk business," I told him with a straight face. When it was time to talk figures a nigga like me kept my poker face on.

Twenty minutes later, Santa and I had come to an agreement on how much kush I was about to supply him with and how much I was about to get for it.

Did I feel bad that I was fresh out of jail and back to my old ways that landed me there in the first place? No, I wasn't, the way I looked at it. Before I went to prison I was more hands on with my operations. Meaning I used to distribute my product to the local block boys to sell and they ran my money each week. But with that type of operation you always run the risks of niggas stealing your shit.

There was always a motherfucker that wasn't happy, there was always a motherfucker that thought he should be eating better than others in the crew. I couldn't deal with that shit, so I did my research on who would be willing to buy my entire stash from me.

Of course, it was always those white boys or Colombians that dealt with moving weight on that magnitude. I didn't mind, and I knew that was the direction I was willing to go. I wanted to cut the middle man out completely.

"Hey, if you know of anyone that would be interested in the best Jamaican kush on the market, tell them get at me," I said as I stood up to leave.

"Actually, there is somebody who might like to take you up on that offer. Matter of fact, he should be here any minute, so stick around and let me introduce you both." I thought about for a minute because I was always sceptical about meeting people I didn't know, especially under these types of circumstances.

"I'on know man," I began to say, but Santa's cell began ringing just then and he reached on the glass table at the centre of the room and picked it up.

"Hello," he said as he answered his call.

I stood waiting for him to end his call, listening as he told the person on the other end that he would be right there, before he hung up his phone.

"You're in luck. You're about to meet the person I believe would be more than interested in getting in on the grade of product you got. Have a seat, let me go let him in." Santa turned and walked away as fast as his huge self could walk and I sat as I was instructed to do.

I looked around as I rubbed on my beard, thinking to myself about the real reason I chose Santa to do business with in the first place. I really wanted to find out what his affiliation was with Sammie's husband.

I couldn't just blurt it out on the very first meeting I had with him. Nah, I had to get this big bellied motherfucker to have a little trust in me first. I had to get him to warm up to me a little then I would somehow bring Adam up. My gut was telling me that nigga was full of nothing but bullshit.

I heard Santa making his way back to where I was seated as he spoke to whomever he just let into his home. I honestly wasn't interested in meeting anyone else because that's not the way I did business. It's hard trusting people in this drug world.

One bad choice of a buyer and that motherfucker could try to double cross you.

When they entered the room I turned to them and I couldn't believe my fucking luck. Santa walked up to where I sat with his company following him with an expression that read he wished the earth could open and swallow his ass up.

"Kingsale Rock, I'd like for you to meet Taye Diggs." I almost choked on my spit when Santa introduced Sammie's husband as Taye Diggs. For a smart drug lord, Santa sure was stupid. But in his defense he was white man that lived in a very upscale neck of the woods. He had no idea what us black folks where doing on the opposite side of his bougie community. But knowing him, I didn't think he would have given a rat's ass who the fuck Adam was any fucking way.

Hence the reason why he had no idea that he had been selling drugs to a very well known and respected councillor for the ghetto. Also, I was pretty certain Santa never saw a Taye Diggs movie in his entire life.

"Mr. Diggs, it's a pleasure to meet you," I said as I stood with an outstretched hand for Adam to shake. I smiled as I saw his jaw twitch in anger as he shook my hand almost in a robotic manner.

"Mr. Rock, it's good to meet you," Adam said as he pulled his hand away from mine. He was injecting daggers into my eyeballs as he glared at me, his anger very imminent. I was un-moved by his rage as I smiled in his face.

"I was telling my friend here about the grade of marijuana you supply, Kingsale. I think you should consider joining forces with him. You could trust him, Kingsale. I've been doing business with him for quite some time now." Santa was such a clueless motherfucker, it was almost comical. He was giving me exactly the information that I wanted, and I loved it.

"Let's not keep Mr. Rock back. He looks as though he was about to leave," Adam said, an expressionless look on his face as he continued to stare at me.

"Yes, I was about to leave. But if you have interest in doing business with me I wouldn't mind that at all. You could always pass word on to Santa, and he would get in touch with me. You know you look very familiar, have we ever met before?" I asked, just to fuck with him.

"I can't say that we know each other," he replied.

"Hmm, maybe you just have one of those faces then. Anyway, Santa, until we meet again for the drop off." Santa and I shook hands before I gave Adam one final look before I turned and walked out of the room.

As I tossed the hood of my jacket over my head as I walked outside, I smiled triumphantly. I just knew there was something off with that nigga. He talked a whole lot of shit about keeping his community clean and drug free and here he was having a meeting with one of the most notorious drug lords.

As I walked to my car I couldn't quite understand how I didn't know about Adam and his connections to the streets. Since he was using the ridiculous name of a famous actor with Santa, I was certain he had an alias in the streets also.

As I drove away from the lavish house and made my way home, I knew I was now officially out of a job. I didn't mind that one bit. The only negative of that would be not seeing Sammie as often as I would like from now on.

I had a plan, however, on getting her on my side and getting her to leave her two-faced husband once and for all. I could give a fuck if I had to snitch on that nigga and let her know who she was really married to... Samantha Daniel would one day soon be Samantha Rock!

I was about to make sure of that.

Adam Daniel

This stupid motherfucker Santa! I swear if he didn't have a house full of bodyguards I would have pulled my gun out and popped two in the middle of his forehead.

I gripped the steering wheel of my car tight as fuck as I drove home. My knuckles were beginning to turn white as I focused on the road.

My mind was spinning around and around, with thoughts on how I was about to iron out this situation that was tossed in my face. Well I knew for damn sure the first thing would be to fire King.

I thought giving him this job was enough to keep him from dealing, seeing that I was paying him more than he was worth anyway. But nah, that nigga was back to his old tricks again selling in the streets and fucking up my money.

So maybe I wasn't the type of nigga I portrayed to the public but tell me who the fuck was! Show me a motherfucker that lived his life being constantly scrutinized by the public and he was actually that nigga everyone thought he was?

I mean, I enjoyed my job as being a councillor and everything, but that shit wasn't enough to afford me the type of life I wanted. Not when you grew up dirt poor like I did in the roughest part of the projects.

I heard gunshots every single day as if that shit was normal. I saw drug dealers and crack-heads every single time I left my house. I was the only child to a man that loved a woman way more than she loved him.

My mother was nothing but hood rat trash, who didn't deserve my father on her worst day. She used her big booty and voluptuous curves to lure other men when she was supposed to be a married woman. My father made an honest living driving a bus, so he didn't make a lot of money which was a huge problem for my mother.

I never heard that woman do anything but complain about my father and what he couldn't give her. She never had one thing good to say about him more than he was a lousy husband and she wished she never married him.

My dad refused to give up on the woman he loved; he believed that one day she would change back to the thoughtful woman he married. The way he loved my mother was mind boggling, even after he found out she had cheated on him with multiple niggas in our community. He never left her.

Growing up in the hood, I had the pleasure of seeing all my neighbours and classmates sell weed, cocaine and crack. I saw them rock designer wear, gold chains, and new rides, all while I wore shoes with holes in the soles.

I was jealous of their lifestyle and the expensive shit they rocked and aspired to be like them one day. My father definitely couldn't afford Fubu and Phat Farm clothing on a bus driver's salary.

Then when I was about thirteen years old the unthinkable happened; my mother left us. I'm talking about left us like we meant absolutely nothing to her. She came home one night from being out with her friends, looked my father right in his eyes and told him she was leaving him.

I remember my father begged her to stay, saying he would take another job, or request that he work extra shifts on his bus driving. All that he said wasn't enough for that selfish bitch. She told him she met somebody that could afford her the type of life she thought she deserved. She packed up all her stuff and left that night, never to be heard from again.

I, for one, was happy that she left, that way she couldn't hurt my father anymore. From that day onward, I vowed I'd never fall in love with women who reminded me of or looked anything like my mother. Which was the reason that I fucked women only of different races; y'all can keep those big booty hood bitches for all I care.

With my mother gone and my dad being on the road driving his bus, I used to have way too much free time any thirteen-year-old should have. Before long, I ended up on the block with the other no good niggas, selling weed.

I was finally able to afford the brand name clothing and expensive jewelry just as everyone else. That hood rich lifestyle didn't last long since my father soon found out what I was doing when he found a shoebox filled with cash and gold jewelry hidden under my bed.

I wasn't too old to get my ass whopped and from then on out he never let me out of his sight. I had to accompany him on his afternoon bus rides, and he showed me as we drove through our poverty-stricken streets how many people were strung out on drugs.

On one of those very bus rides one day, my father made me promise that I should never add to the problems black people face every day. He told me instead of being part of the problem I should find a solution.

That shit changed me. I stopped hanging out on the block, stopped selling weed and other drugs, and studied my ass off in school. That shit paid off and a nigga got a scholarship to one of the most prom-inent colleges out of state.

I came back and pursued my dream of being a councillor for the community I grew up in. I had big ambitions when I started this job six years ago. Unfortunately, my father passed the same time I got this job. I learned quickly that this job had certain perks to it, dealing with an underground circle of everything from crooked cops, to dirty politicians and judges. Before I knew what was happening, I was quickly sucked back into the drug world.

I knew about King way longer than that nigga knew about me, all because he was fucking up my money. When he started dealing his block boys were selling out way faster than my crew. He was taking my regular customers and my product was moving way too slow for my liking.

So if he was back in the game again, he would once again be fucking with my money...and I couldn't have that. I was able to put him away for those two years he spent inside. When I found out he got arrested I called in a little favor to the judge that was seeing about his case and he got three years, even though he didn't serve his full sentence.

My phone rang bringing me out of reverie. I looked at the screen and thought on whether I should bother answering it or not.

I exhaled softly before I swiped on the screen.

"Hey, Sandy," I said as I pulled my car onto the street I lived on.

"Aren't you coming over to see us today?" she asked, as I cursed myself softly because I had completely forgotten that I promised her that I would stop by before I made it home.

"Look, something came up and I won't be able to swing through. I'll be sure to drop in on you guys tomorrow," I said, apologizing to her even though I really didn't need to.

"Really, Adam? So you just gonna do me like that," Sandy said, being her usual dramatic self. I shook my head at her as I pulled up in front of my house, making my way down the driveway.

"What I just say, Sandy? I'll swing through tomorrow." I put some extra bass in my voice to let her ass know that I wasn't playing. I heard her suck her teeth loudly.

"Don't make me call your wife, Adam," she said to me in a threatening tone, but all that did was make me mad as hell.

"You better gone with that bullshit. Don't ever threaten to call my wife, Sandy. I'll make your money hungry ass regret you've ever been born. Like I said, I'll be by tomorrow." Not giving her a chance to reply, seeing how she pissed me all the way off, I ended the call on her ass.

The story of how I met Sandy would come at a later time; right now I needed to let my wife know that we needed to look for a new driver. I could see that she enjoyed King working for us, but too bad his uncle had already returned to his home country, or I would not have hesitated to give him his old job back.

I got out my car and made my way to the front door letting myself in. I walked through the living room and made my way to the kitchen, admiring my home as I did.

I was so proud of what I had accomplished in the forty-three years I'd been on this earth. This house was one I could have only dreamed about even after having a job as a councillor. This house was purchased with the help of running my own drug block.

Peeping into the kitchen, I was surprised that I didn't see Samantha waiting in there for me. She normally sat in the kitchen waiting on my return so she could dish out a hot meal for me. I looked at a single plate that was laid out, covered down on the counter.

I walked to it and lifted the plastic lid that covered it and saw that it was my dinner. Replacing the lid, I turned and made my way up the stairs to our bedroom. I opened the door and found my wife sitting on the bed watching television.

She paid me no mind as I walked inside of the bedroom and shut the door. I looked up at the screen to see that she was looking at the Food Network channel; she loved looking at that channel.

"Hey," I said as I began undressing.

"Hey," was all she said as she replied to me, still not looking in my direction. I knew my wife may think that I didn't love her, but in reality I actually did love her in my own special way. She was a wonderful woman and I knew for a fact that I didn't deserve her.

After all the shit I done put her through, I knew she deserved a much better husband than I ever was to her. I kept promising myself that I would do right by her one day, treat her the way she deserved. But sometimes when I looked at her she reminded me of my mother. That shit creeped me the fuck out, especially since Samantha gained some weight recently.

Her butt got bigger, her hips got wider, her legs got thicker. The same way my momma used to look. I just felt that Samantha would probably use her new curvaceous body the same way my momma did.

That's why I'd been on her to lose the weight so much. I hated to think that men would lust after her body.

"I think I'll be firing, Kingsale." This got her attention as she snapped her head in my direction to look at me.

"What? For what, why do you feel the need to fire him?" she asked, with a worried expression on her face.

"I have reason to believe that he stole from me the other day," I said, lying as I looked her straight in her eyes.

"Stole from you? King would never steal from you, Adam." *Now hold up just one motherfucking minute!* I thought as I paused from taking my shirt off.

"King? Why you calling him that? You have a pet name for our driver now?" I was almost tempted to smack her right across her face. I could tell she looked slightly embarrassed by the fact that she called him by a pet name.

"He asked me to call him that. So you can stop looking at me like that and explain as to why you think he stole from you," she said, as she muted the volume on the TV. I wasn't fully satisfied with that answer but for now, I decided to let it slide.

"I purposely left some money in the car the other day when he drove me around. You know, as a way to test his honesty, and when I got back in the car the money was gone." Samantha wrinkled her forehead as she stared at me with a doubtful look on her face.

"But that doesn't make any sense. It would be pretty obvious that he would know that you would suspect him. Are you sure you didn't just misplace the money?" I had to say I wasn't enjoying the fact that she seemed to be taking Kingsale's side over mine.

"No, I didn't misplace the money, Samantha! Kingsale took it," I shouted out at her, and she physically cowered back from me. I hadn't even realized that I had walked closer to her where she sat on the bed.

"OK, Adam, if you think that's the best solution, go ahead and fire him," she said as she looked away from me. I noticed the bruise on her forehead, knowing that was my doing, and sat next to her on the bed.

"Look, I know you may have taken to Kingsale over the past week but I'll get you a replacement as soon as I can." I massaged her shoulders as I tried to convince her but she didn't even bother to look my way. The next thing that came out of my mouth took Samantha by surprise but it also had me wondering what the fuck was I thinking when I said it.

"I think it's time we work on having a baby." Samantha's head spun around with a quickness as she stared at me with her mouth wide open.

"What?" she said softly, as she waited for me repeat what I said. I couldn't help but smile at the way those words made her so happy. I tenderly touched the bruised spot on her forehead and bent and kissed her lips.

"Let's have a baby. I know that would make you the happiest wife in the world, right?" I asked her, as she smiled back at me and nodded her head enthusiastically. "We'll go to the doctor and make sure everything's all good and within the next few months you'll be waddling around this house with a big old belly." Samantha shrieked in excitement as she threw herself into me, wrapping her arms around my neck.

Was I serious about having a baby? To be honest, I wasn't, but Samantha had been a good wife all these years and I knew I had been a shitty husband. The way I saw it, this was the least I could do for her. I knew she had been wanting to have a baby for a while now.

"I'm so happy, Adam. I hope we get a little girl so that I could dress her up and show her off to everybody," she gushed as she climbed up on her knees and she held onto my hand.

I was low-key glad that she forgot all about Kingsale and the fact that I had to fire him, even though I lied about the circumstances.

As Samantha and I looked at each other, it suddenly dawned on me that I couldn't even remember the last time we even had sex. The longer I thought about it the harder it was for me to recollect when was the last time I had sex with my wife.

Was I that caught up with fucking Sandy and entertaining a few escorts every now again, that I had no clue when was the last time I was inside my wife?

Then this brought on another thought, what the fuck did she do for pleasure? It could have been well over three months, I believed it could have been, since we'd been intimate. Samantha never showed interest in having me touch her...hmmmm.

"Let's start now," I told her, and she seemed a bit thrown off by what I just said.

"What do you mean?" she asked, just as I reached over to her and tugged the straps of the dress she was wearing down past her shoulders.

"I mean, let's start practicing to have this baby right now, Samantha." I saw a flicker of uncertainty in her eyes but it quickly faded and she bent to capture my lips with hers.

"Ok," she said, wasting no time to lift her dress above her head, tossing it on the bed. I pulled her onto my lap as she got comfortable in a straddling position.

This was just a small distraction of what I knew I would have to deal with eventually. King knew about my secret life and even though I would be getting rid of him by firing him, I couldn't be too sure if he would spill my secret life to anyone.

I had absolutely no plans on the public finding out that I had been living a lie all this time. I also had no plans on letting him fuck with my money.

As my hands roamed over my wife's voluptuous body, I silently decided right then and there that if Kingsale became a problem of any kind...

I had no problem putting an end to his reign as King!

King

uck that nigga Adam Daniel! That motherfucker actually had the nerve to call me up, talking 'bout I'm fired.

I was like, nah nigga, I quit. Fuck you mean!

I pulled hard on my blunt I held between my fingers, as I sat in my deathly quiet living room. The place had to be really still when I was deep in thought.

The smoke from my blunt clouded my vision as I thought about what Adam said to me because quite frankly, it was kind of bothering me.

After I told his stupid ass I quit because I didn't even want that fuck job in the first place, I only took it to be closer to Sammie. But after telling him I quit he said, *good, now let me go back to fucking my wife.*

That shit that he said made my stomach do a few somersaults. Sammie told me, as a matter of fact Sammie swore to me, that she and her husband stopped having sex a few months ago.

She swore that he was too busy entertaining other females and that he hadn't touched her since we both started having sex. I even told her ass that she wasn't allowed to let that nigga touch her. I didn't give a fuck how crazy and stupid it may have sounded. I told her ass that nigga wasn't allowed to touch her; I didn't care what she had to do. She could have told him she had crabs for all I cared.

I didn't know if he said that shit just to get a rise out of me but it sure the hell worked... I was motherfucking livid.

I would be getting to the bottom of it real soon though because Sammie was on her way over here. She called me this morning saying that we had to talk, and I assumed it had to do with the fact that her *batty boy* husband fired my ass. I was curious as to the explanation he gave her for my dismissal though. I couldn't wait for her to tell me the lie he told her.

I pulled the blunt from my lips and looked at it. This fucking kush was off the motherfucking chain. I began feeling high already and I just now started smoking this shit.

I started having second thoughts about supplying the shipment of weed I received to Santa. Since I found out that Sammie's husband was chin deep in running his own weight in the streets, I began doing some research on who he was known as in the hood.

I came up with nothing though, but you best believe I would be finding out sooner rather than later exactly the type of clout this nigga had on the streets.

Since I began having second thoughts about dealing with Santa, I decided I was about to get my boys back out on the blocks hustling for me. I was about to run councilman Adam Daniel's pockets dry.

There was a soft knock at my front door and I made my way over to answer it. I didn't even bother to get dressed since Sammie told me she was coming over. I knew we would end up in my bed, or the floor, or the shower fucking each other's brains out eventually anyways. So I just wore a pair of grey sweatpants with nothing else.

I opened the door for her and smiled when I caught sight of my baby; she was so fine.

"My Empress," I said, as I dipped my head so that I could peck her on her lips. I moved to the side and allowed her to step inside. I couldn't quite put my finger on it, but she seemed different...and not in a good way.

"You good?" I asked as I pulled on my blunt, as I studied her nervous body language.

"Yeah, can we have a seat so we can talk?" she said as she fiddled with her fingers. Oh yeah, something was definitely up with her. Not saying anything, I took her hand in mine and led her over to my sofa.

We sat next to each other and she turned to look at me with doubt in her eyes.

"I guess your husband already told you that he tried to fire me. I turned that shit around on him real quick and told him I quit." Sammie got a somewhat confused look on her face.

"Why would you steal his money, King?" she said that shit the exact same time I pulled on my blunt and a nigga started choking. I had to put the blunt out as I thumped hard on my chest, swearing I was about to die.

"That nigga said what?" I asked as I put my head closer to her mouth, because I knew damn well I had heard her wrong.

"He said he left money in his car when you drove him around the other day and when he came back the money was gone." I pulled my head back so that I could look her in her eyes because she sounded as though she believed in that lie her husband told her.

"Nah, fuck what he said. Do you think I stole that nigga's money?" I asked as I curled my upper lip, sneering at her, as I pointed my index finger in her face.

"I told him you had no reason to take his money and that he probably misplaced it. I don't see you as a thief, King. You know that." I narrowed my eyes at her ready to go the fuck off and let her know her husband was nothing but a lying, no good nigga who was more than likely running his own drug block.

I was mad as fuck that he tried to pass me off as a petty thief. My chest was rising and falling as I opened my mouth to let her know who she was really married to.

Before I got the chance to do that, my eyes fell on her neck and a nigga had to do a double take. Not even thinking about it, I reached up and roughly grabbed the side of her face as I tilted her head to one side.

"The fuck is that, Sammie?!" I asked as I shouted at her, as my eyes glared at the hickey she was sporting on her neck. That motherfucker looked fresh too, as if she fucked just before she came over here.

"King, that's what I came over here to talk to you about." I knew she spoke but at the moment, everything sounded like gibberish as I continued to stare at the love bite on her neck.

"Yo, who put that hickey on your neck Sammie?" I said with my teeth clenched tightly as I gripped her chin even harder.

"Stop, King, you're hurting my face, let go," she complained as she tried to wriggle her face free, but I held on tight refusing to let go.

"Answer my motherfucking question, Sammie. Who put that hickey on your neck?"

"Are you forgetting I'm a married woman, King." Her words stung as if she had just shot me straight through my heart. I pulled my hand away instantly and just stared at her in silence.

"Oh, word. So it's like that, Sammie? All that...me and my husband don't even have sex was all bullshit? I guess I was nothing more than a big fucking joke to you huh?" I shook my head feeling as though I was about to snap. I needed to move away from Sammie, put some safe distance between us before I wrapped my hands around her throat and choked the shit out of her.

I walked to the opposite side of where she sat and shoved my hands in my sweatpants pocket. Sammie and I looked at each other for a few seconds, neither saying anything, before she finally spoke up.

"Adam seems to want to make our marriage work. He says we should try to start a family." With my hands planted deep inside my pockets, I tilted my head back as I narrowed my eyes listening to her words.

Seeing that I wasn't about to reply, she continued talking. "I don't want you to think that what we shared didn't mean anything to me. It did, King, I just want you to know that. You meant so much to me but Adam is my husband and I should try and make things work with him." I listened as I balled up my hands into fists but kept them in my pockets.

"King, what were we doing really? What did we have? It was just nothing more than great sex. How could we possibly be together? You being younger than me was somewhat of an issue for me and you knew it."

"It wasn't an issue when I was running up in your guts, re-arranging your inner organs. Me being younger was no problem then, right, Sammie? What we had was nothing more than great sex, really? After all this time that's how you looked at what we had, that we were just fucking?" Hearing her say that shit made my heart drop to my feet. I cared about this woman more than she could ever know.

Sammie had no idea how much she affected my life since the very first night I saw her. There wasn't a day that went by that I never thought about her. But here she was looking at me dead in my eyes and telling me I was nothing more than a play thing to her.

"I'm sorry, but I want nothing more than to start a family with the man I married, King. Please try and understand that," she said, as she stood up and made her way over to where I stood.

"Don't even think to come any closer to me. Get the fuck out my house, Sammie." She paused immediately and looked at me as if what I said had her stunned. I didn't see why it should.

"King, ple—"

"What, you slow now?" I asked, interrupting whatever it was she was about to say. "I said, get...the...fuck...out...my...house." I spaced my words out just in case she was hard of hearing as she was pretending to be.

Sighing loudly, she opened her handbag and pulled out an envelope. "I think it's only fair that I give this back to you," she said, as she held out the envelope I gave her a few days ago with the money for her yoga studio.

I didn't even attempt to take it from out of her hand, so she placed it on the sofa.

"I also wanted to return this to you. I think it's the right time." She dipped in her handbag once again, this time taking an item out that I hadn't worn for the past two years.

Like the envelope, she placed my iced-out gold chain with the King pendant on the sofa and faced me.

"If I hurt you in any way, please believe me when I say it was never my intention." Once again, the thought of wringing her neck crossed my mind and I turned to walk to the front door so that I could let her ass out.

I opened the door and stood to the side as Sammie slowly made her way toward the door to make her exit.

As she walked out, the words passed my lips before it registered in my head. "I can't wait for you to find out who you really married to."

She paused out the door with a confused look on her face, and I believed she was about to say something. To bad for her though because I slammed the door in her face instead.

With legs that wanted nothing more than to turn and go after her, these legs turned around instead and walked back into the living room. I picked the envelope of money up as well as my chain and walked inside of my bedroom.

Tossing the envelope on the bed, I made my way to my full-length mirror and stared at the reflection that looked back at me.

So this was the thanks I got for caring about a female; I got a swift kick in my ass. She's going to go and try and make things work with a nigga she didn't really know.

I looked away from my reflection at the chain that I held in my hand, then I looked back at myself in the mirror.

After a few minutes of staring at myself, I realized I needed to get back in the game.

"Fuck that bitch," I mumbled as I placed the chain around my neck as it dangled against my naked stomach.

With an expression as cold as ice, I stared at myself in the mirror and nodded my head.

The King was back in the game. I was about to reclaim my motherfucking throne and take back these streets.

To be continued...........................

TO MY READERS

Hi guys, I hoped you all enjoyed reading about King and Samantha. This book was another attempt of a standalone...lolol, but once again that didn't turn out too well. As always, I love hearing from you all so when you're done, please leave me a review and let me know what you think. What would you like to see happen in part 2? Did you all enjoy reading Selah's story, would you like to see her end up with her sexy boss?

Sound off in the reviews because you guys' input is so important to me!

Royalty Publishing House is now accepting manuscripts from aspiring or experienced urban romance authors!

WHAT MAY PLACE YOU ABOVE THE REST:

Heroes who are the ultimate book bae: strong-willed, maybe a little rough around the edges but willing to risk it all for the woman he loves.

Heroines who are the ultimate match: the girl next door type, not perfect - has her faults but is still a decent person. One who is willing to risk it all for the man she loves.

The rest is up to you! Just be creative, think out of the box, keep it sexy and intriguing!

If you'd like to join the Royal family, send us the first 15K words (60 pages) of your completed manuscript to submissions@royaltypublish-inghouse.com

LIKE OUR PAGE!

Be sure to <u>LIKE</u> our Royalty Publishing House page on Facebook!

CPSIA information can be obtained
at www.ICGtesting.com
Printed in the USA
LVHW041717060219
606614LV00002B/242/P